Just Grace and the
Flower Girl Power

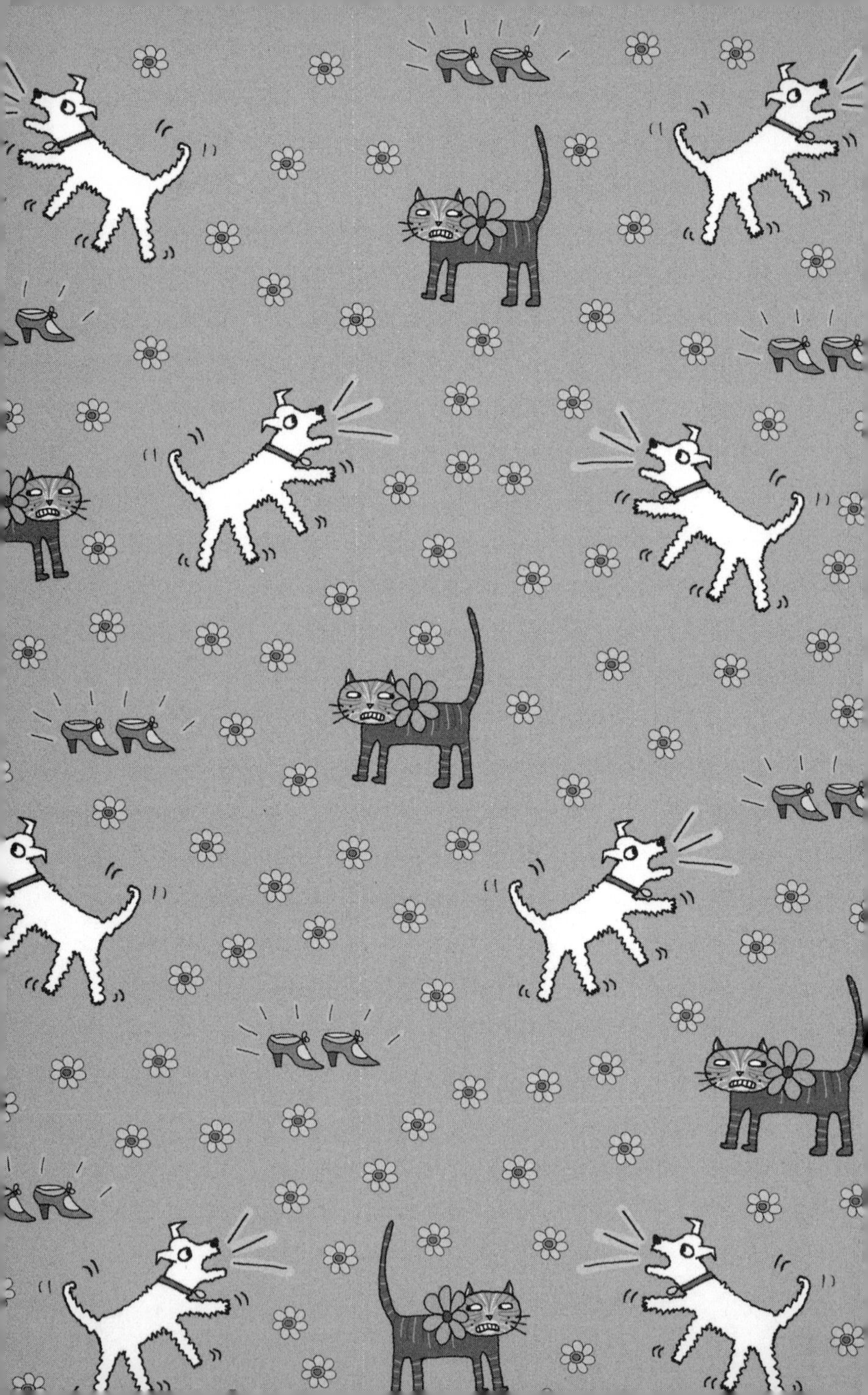

Just Grace and the Flower Girl Power

Written and illustrated
by

Charise Mericle Harper

sandpiper

Houghton Mifflin Harcourt
Boston New York

All rights reserved. Published in the United States by Sandpiper, an imprint of
Houghton Mifflin Harcourt Publishing Company. Originally published in hardcover
in the United States by Houghton Mifflin Books for Children, an imprint of
Houghton Mifflin Harcourt Publishing Company, 2012.

SANDPIPER and the SANDPIPER logo are trademarks of Houghton Mifflin
Harcourt Publishing Company.

www.hmhbooks.com

The text of this book is set in Dante MT.
The illustrations are pen-and-ink drawings digitally colored in Photoshop.

The Library of Congress has cataloged the hardcover edition as follows:
Harper, Charise Mericle.
Just Grace and the flower girl power / written and illustrated by Charise
Mericle Harper.
p. cm.
[1. Weddings—Fiction.] I. Title.
PZ7.H231323Jth 2011
[Fic]—dc23
2011039908

ISBN 978-0-547-57720-3 hardcover
ISBN: 978-0-544-02283-6 paperback

Manufactured in the United States of America
DOC 10 9 8 7 6 5 4 3 2 1
4500400772

Thank you, Penny and Pepper!

THE FIVE BIG I·CAN NOT·BELIEVE·ITS OF MY LIFE SO FAR

1. That my teacher, Miss Lois, decided to call me Just Grace instead of my real name, which is Grace, without the Just part in front of it. This happened a while ago, but it still bugs me! Even just thinking about it can make me grumpy. Yesterday I drew a cartoon explaining how the whole thing happened. Sometimes drawing cartoons helps me feel better. I don't know why it works, but it does. I'm glad about that.

2. That I finally got a real live pet, and it's NOT a turtle or a fish! A while ago I had a big idea to make a pretend dog. I called him Chip-Up and I made him out of cardboard boxes. I took care of him like he was real. That way Mom and Dad could see how responsible I was and then they'd let me get a real dog. Chip-Up looked super good, and even though I worked really hard to take care of him, Dad did not seem like he was ever going to turn into a dog-loving person. But one day he surprised me and did. The day I got Mr. Scruffers was the best day of my entire life! A cardboard dog is okay, but a real dog is 100 percent better.

And even though Mr. Scruffers is a girl dog and has a boy name, she is still amazing and perfect for me!

3. That Augustine Dupre is getting married in two weeks and I didn't even know she had a boyfriend.

THINGS I KNEW
FRENCH FURNITURE
NICE CLOTHES
LOVE FOR CRINKLES
FANCY DISHES
AUGUSTINE DUPRE HAD

4. That Augustine Dupre is having her wedding in the middle of Mrs. Luther's backyard. Mrs. Luther is one of my next-door neighbors, so if I wanted to, I could spy on the wedding and see the whole thing right from my bedroom window. Of course I am 100 percent invited to the wedding, so the

spying part doesn't matter, but still even just knowing that I could do it is kind of cool.

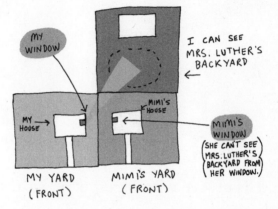

5. That I am NOT going to be the flower girl at Augustine Dupre's wedding!

FIVE THINGS ABOUT AUGUSTINE DUPRE THAT YOU CANNOT TELL BY JUST LOOKING AT HER

1. She is a very good listener. If there is something you want to say, she can make the air

around her quiet and still so the words just float out of your mouth without you even having to think about pushing them.

2. She is in love with Mrs. Luther's cat, Crinkles. Even though Crinkles lives next door with Mrs. Luther, he spends a lot of time visiting with Augustine Dupre and sitting on her sofa.

3. She has great ideas and is a good problem solver. She can make an idea go straight from her head into your head so easily that your brain might even forget that she thought of it first.

4. She is funny and likes to make jokes.

5. She is my best grown-up friend who is not related to me.

WHAT I DID TWO SECONDS AFTER AUGUSTINE DUPRE TOLD ME SHE WAS GETTING MARRIED

I screamed. "AAAAAAHHHHHHHHHH-HHHHHH!" It was a long, happy scream, so Augustine Dupre was mostly surprised and not mostly scared. That was good. I couldn't help the scream. Sometimes you can't help but be crazy if your head is suddenly feeling combustible. The extra energy has to get out of there somehow.

WHAT HAPPENED TEN SECONDS AFTER AUGUSTINE DUPRE TOLD ME SHE WAS GETTING MARRIED

My brain went through a superfast list of everything to do with a wedding: wedding dress, flowers, flower girl . . . and then it stopped. I looked up at Augustine Dupre and said, "I will be the best flower girl ever! I promise! I promise! I promise!" And then I threw my hands into the air and said it one more time, extra big for special meaning: "I PROMISE!"

WHAT IS SAD BUT TRUE

Just because you really, really, really want be
a flower girl and you know you'd be perfect
at it, and even if it's probably the only time in
your entire life that you'll have the chance to
be one, this does not mean that your wish of
being the flower girl is going to come true.
This I did not know.

HOW I FOUND OUT ABOUT NOT BEING THE FLOWER GIRL

I opened my arms to give Augustine Dupre
a big I'm-so-happy-I-get-to-be-the-flower-girl
hug, but instead of letting me hug her she
held my hands and looked down at me with
a sad face. "Oh, Grace! I'm so sorry," she said.
"You can't be the flower girl. Luke has promised being the flower girl to his little cousin.
We'll find something else for you to do. I

promise! Something special." Augustine Dupre was saying lots of words, but the only ones
that I was hearing over and over again were
"You can't be the flower girl. You can't be the
flower girl. You can't be the flower girl."

It was surprising, because even though I had

only been thinking I was going
to be the flower girl for about
two minutes, it was still super
disappointing and sad to find
out it wasn't going to happen.

WHAT MY BRAIN WAS THINKING NEXT

WHAT MY MOUTH SAID NEXT

"What's her name? The girl who gets to be the flower girl?" I don't know why it was important, but suddenly I wanted to know everything about her. It was 100 percent easy for me to imagine that I was not going to like her even one teeny tiny bit.

Augustine Dupre looked worried. Probably because I was wearing my unhappy face—sometimes I'm not very good at hiding it. She made a little sigh and said, "Her name is Delphine. She's five years old and she is Luke's only niece. I'm sure you will like her, and I know she will love you!" Augustine Dupre put her hands on my shoulders and studied my eyes like she was trying to see into my brain to know what I was thinking. It was a good thing she didn't have those kind of powers. Sometimes the things that go on inside your head are better kept private.

WORDS CAN BE POWERFUL

I don't know why it happened, but suddenly my whole mood was different. Augustine Dupre's words had changed me. She had changed my mad to sad.

Mad is easier than sad.
Sadness is not easy.

WHAT WAS NOT AN EXCELLENT SUGGESTION

"Maybe you can help Delphine practice," said Augustine Dupre. "She will need some help. What do you think?"

WHY THIS WAS NOT AN EXCELLENT IDEA

I looked up at Augustine Dupre and smiled. I gave her my best fake smile— the one I had practiced tons of times. It worked great for the school photo, and I

I DON'T WANT TO HELP HER DO A GOOD JOB.

NOT REAL SMILE

wanted it to work on Augustine Dupre too. I didn't want her to be sad. Being a bride is super special. It's the only time a grown-up girl gets to be like a princess. Lucky for me, I'm really good at the smile—it worked. So far Mom's the only one who can tell it's not for real.

THE SMILES

NOT REAL   REAL

WHAT IS NOT EASY

It's not easy to think of the exact right thing to say when someone is looking at you and expecting you to say the exact right thing. And what I didn't want to do was to say something wrong and ruin Augustine Dupre's bride-happiness.

WHAT I SAID

I took a deep breath, looked up at Augustine Dupre, and said, "I might have a lot of homework. I don't know yet, but I'll really try, you know, to be helpful."

Augustine Dupre smiled and opened her arms for the hug from before. "Of course, Grace," she said. "I know you'll do your best. It's going to be fun. You'll see." I hugged her back real tight. Sometimes a hug can say things that a mouth just can't.

WHAT MY HUG WAS SAYING EVEN
THOUGH I WAS NOT TALKING

I had a few more questions for Augustine Dupre before I ran upstairs to tell Mom the wedding news. She was going to be crazy surprised.

WHAT I COULD NOT BELIEVE

I couldn't believe that Augustine Dupre was going to be marrying someone I had never even met before. That part was weird—really weird.

MY QUESTIONS
1. Who is Luke?
2. Does he live in France?
3. Is he going to visit soon?
4. Does he speak English?

As soon as I finished asking my questions, Augustine Dupre's hands shot up to her mouth. It was wide open. She was shocked. "But, Grace," she said, "you've met him. How can you not know Luke?" She held up a you-wait-here finger, then turned and ran off into her kitchen. From the doorway I could see her pull something off the fridge. I was patient and still, but she ran back anyway, like maybe she was worried I was going to leave or something. "Look," she said. She held out a long piece of paper. It was a photo strip from an automatic photo machine—the kind where it's fun to make all sorts of silly faces. "There," she said, and she pointed to one of the pictures. A smiling man was

posing next to her. "You know Luke, right?" she asked. I squinted. He looked familiar, but somehow my brain just couldn't remember from where. Dumb brain!

WHAT IS UNFORTUNATE

Just because there is an easy way to solve a problem, it does not mean that you will be smart enough to choose that way. The smart me would have said, "Augustine Dupre, can you help me remember where I know Luke from?" And even though I would have maybe been embarrassed for a second, she would have for sure helped me.

But I did not do this. Instead, I pretended that I remembered that I knew him. It saved me from being embarrassed, but now I was stuck in a yes-I-know-Luke lie!

AUGUSTINE DUPRE'S BOYFRIEND

When someone shows you a picture of their almost-husband, you should really offer up some compliments. It's super bad manners not to say something nice—even I know that. "He's very smiley," I said. "And I like this picture too." I pointed to the one where they were both sticking out their tongues. Augustine Dupre smiled. It was a real smile, I could tell, because of her eyes.

TWINKLE IN HER EYE

WHAT MOM SAID WHEN I TOLD HER ABOUT THE WEDDING

"I know! Isn't it exciting?" Mom did a twirl and started humming the wedding song. "Da dum da da. Da dum da—" I couldn't believe it! "Mom!" I shouted. "You knew about the wedding? How come you didn't tell me?" Mom stopped in the middle of her second twirl. "Sweetie, Augustine Dupre wanted to be the one to tell you. It's her big news, not mine." She came and hugged me. Weirdly, today was turning out to be a big day for hugging.

WHAT MOM SAID NEXT

"I know it's a change, but it's a happy change, right?" Mom was still hugging me tight. She was waiting for an answer. I could tell I was trapped. Her arms were like padlocks of love—they were only going to open if she knew I was feeling okay. I nodded my head yes. It worked. She gave me an extra squeeze and then let go. "Hey," said Mom. "How about some French toast? Would you like that?" "No thank you," I said. "I'll have cereal." "Okay," said Mom. "If that makes you happy."

WHY CEREAL CAN MAKE ME HAPPY

THE CEREAL GAME

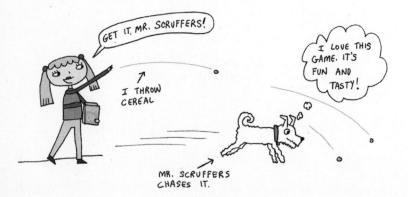

GET IT, MR. SCRUFFERS!

I THROW CEREAL

I LOVE THIS GAME. IT'S FUN AND TASTY!

MR. SCRUFFERS CHASES IT.

After breakfast Mr. Scruffers and I went up to my room, and even though my favorite stuff was all around me, I still couldn't think of a single thing to do.

MY HOUSE AS A HAPPINESS GRAPH

As soon as I got upstairs to my room, I started to think about everything that had just happened. Sometimes doing lots of thinking by yourself is not a good idea. It can make you sad.

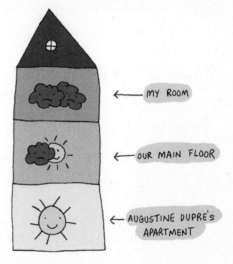

I decided to go down to the living room. The ground floor was closer to Augustine Dupre. Maybe it would help to be closer to her bride-to-be happiness. Maybe some of her joy would float up from the basement and help make me feel better.

LYING ON THE FLOOR

I DON'T FEEL ANYTHING YET.

I didn't have much time to experiment because Mr. Scruffers started whining, jumping on me, and finally racing back and forth between my legs and the back door. She was 100 percent desperate to be let out! There are only two things that make her crazy like that—squirrels and Crinkles.

Mr. Scruffers has a mini-superpower. It

has to do with the backyard. Without even looking out the window or the doorway, she can somehow tell if there is a creature walking around on our lawn. I don't know how she does it.

WHAT I USED TO DO

I used to let Mr. Scruffers charge out the door and chase after a squirrel or Crinkles, but then I started to feel kind of bad. It was my empathy feelings working. And they were working for Crinkles. Suddenly I was thinking about how he must feel super nervous and scared every time he steps into our yard. I'm sure the day we got Mr. Scruffers was one of the worst days of his whole cat life. He really has to be brave to come and visit Augustine Dupre.

MUST BE BRAVE!

HIS LOVE

HOW I HELP CRINKLES

I tried to get Mr. Scruffers not to chase Crinkles, but it's impossible—she has to do it. She can't help herself. It must be a nature thing: dogs can't help but chase cats.

PART THAT MAKES DOGS CHASE CATS.

To help Crinkles I invented a new way for letting Mr. Scruffers outside. First I check out the window to see if Crinkles is out there. If he is, I jiggle the door handle around before I open the door. That way Crinkles can hear the rattle and know what is about to happen. Usually he runs and hides. The extra waiting drives Mr. Scruffers crazy, but at least it's more fair for Crinkles.

RUNS LIKE CRAZY TO HIDE

HEARS DOOR HANDLE

DOESN'T HEAR DOOR HANDLE

WALKS LIKE NORMAL

I don't do the door handle warning for squirrels, but that's okay, because they eat all the strawberries off our strawberry plants. Plus, I don't think they're that scared of Mr. Scruffers anyway. Dad says she'd never catch one in a million years. Squirrels are fast!

WHAT SQUIRRELS MIGHT REALLY BE SAYING

I never really thought about squirrels until we got Mr. Scruffers. Some of her squirrel thinking has rubbed off on me. I don't know for sure, but I have a feeling she spends a lot of time thinking about squirrels.

WHO WAS OUTSIDE

Mr. Scruffers was whining and had her nose pushed right up against the crack where the door opens. I looked out the window to see if it was Crinkles or a squirrel, but I couldn't see anything. Mr. Scruffers was going 100 percent crazy. Finally I just opened the door and followed her out. She ran straight to the side gate. Someone was banging on it and shouting. "Scruffy! Scruffy! Scruffy!"

I didn't have to be a detective to know who it was. It was Robert, Mimi's new little

brother. Robert is in love with Mr. Scruffers—
at least that's what Mimi says. Mr. Scruffers
likes Robert okay, but it's not love, except for
when Robert is eating—then she loves him.

THE TWO IMPORTANT THINGS I SAID TO ROBERT

If you are a dog, food can change everything.

  1. "Robert, you are not allowed to bang on
     the gate. If you want to play with Mr.
     Scruffers, you have to come to the front
     door and ask." I told him this because
     Dad says it's important for people to

not use the side gate. He's worried that someone will leave the gate open and then Mr. Scruffers will get lost. This is a good thing to be worried about. Mostly this is a rule for tall people who can reach the gate latch, but I told Robert about it anyway. It is good practice, because one day he will for sure be taller.

2. "You should probably go home and put on some pants and maybe some shoes." Robert was wearing a T-shirt, racing car underpants, and striped socks. This was not the best choice for an I'm-going-to-play-outside outfit, but maybe when you are almost four years old you don't care so much about pants— you just want to get out of the house really fast!

WHAT HAPPENED NEXT

Robert looked at me and nodded, but he didn't move. It was confusing. Maybe he was only pretending to understand me. Thankfully two seconds later I heard Mimi's voice calling him from her front door. I yelled back at her. "Mimi! He's here!" I didn't want her worrying that he was missing or something. And then I added some more information: "And he's not wearing pants!" Somehow that seemed important. I guess it was, because five seconds later Mimi was suddenly standing in front of us. She was not happy.

ROBERT! I CAN'T BELIEVE THIS.

WHERE ARE YOUR PANTS?

UH...

WHAT ROBERT SAID TO MIMI

"Oops. I forgot."

WHAT MIMI SAID TO ME

"Don't ask. It's a mystery to me too."

WHAT BEST FRIENDS CAN DO

Sometimes best friends can answer each other's questions before the questions are even spoken out loud. This was one of those times.

WHAT I SAID TO MIMI

"Don't worry. I won't tell anyone."

WHAT HAPPENED NEXT

Robert looked down at his legs and up at Mimi, and then he ran back home across the lawn. I guess his brain was thinking, "Oh! I get it. Legs need pants." Whether his brain was also thinking, "Feet need shoes" . . . that part was hard to tell. Mimi followed him home.

WHAT I 100 PERCENT FORGOT TO TELL MIMI

That Augustine Dupre was getting married!

I ran inside and shouted out to Mom that I was going over to Mimi's house.

MOM, I'M GOING OVER TO MIMI'S... AND I'M WEARING PANTS.

WHAT I SAID TO MIMI THE MINUTE SHE OPENED HER DOOR

"Augustine Dupre is getting married in two weeks in Mrs. Luther's backyard, and I don't get to be the flower girl!" Of course Mimi was totally surprised. "You aren't the flower girl? Are you sad or mad?" she asked. "Sad," I said. "And really I should be super happy for Augustine Dupre, but I can't because mostly I'm just sad for me." Mimi made her I-feel-sad-with-you face and opened the door wide so I could come in. I followed her up to her room. On the way we passed the kitchen. She grabbed a plate of banana bread. Mimi is not allowed to take food up to her room, but no one saw her and I didn't say anything. And besides, this was not a normal day. This was a special occasion—it was a flower girl crisis!

WHAT HAPPENED IN MIMI'S ROOM

Of course I had a lot to tell Mimi.

It is impossible to chew and talk at the same time, so by the time I had finished telling Mimi all about the wedding, she had already finished her half of the banana bread. It's easy to chew and listen.

Mimi had lots of questions. Most I could answer, but the last one was a surprise. It was a question I hadn't even thought of before.

CRUMBS

MY HALF OF THE TREAT.

MIMI'S QUESTIONS

1. Are you mad at Augustine Dupre?
2. Are you sure you can't remember who Luke is?
3. Is Luke French? Can he speak English?
4. Are you going to help with Delphine?
5. What special thing are you going to be

doing at the wedding? Did she say what it was?

6. Does Luke like cats? Is he allergic to them?

7. Is Luke going to live with Augustine Dupre in your basement? Or is she going to go live with him?

MY ANSWERS

1. No.

2. I know it's weird, but I can't.

3. Yes. Augustine Dupre says he speaks English perfectly and doesn't even have a French accent.

4. Probably.

5. I don't know. Probably something not exciting.

6. I don't know.

7. OH NO! Do you think she might move away?

WHO CUTELY INTERRUPTED US

I was just starting to get upset, thinking about Augustine Dupre maybe moving away, when someone rattled the handle on Mimi's door. I thought it was Mimi's mom and suddenly a new thought popped into my brain. "Oh no! She'll see my banana bread." I grabbed it off the plate, looked around for a hiding place, and then decided that the best place to hide it was in my mouth. It was a big piece.

Two seconds later Robert opened the door and charged into the room. He ran over to Mimi, flung himself into the air, and landed right beside her on the bed. For a second I thought he might want to cuddle, but suddenly he jumped to his feet and started waving a box in front of her face. "Mimi, open these! Open these! Open these!" he shouted. Mimi took the box from him. "Hey, where

did you get this?" she said. "You aren't supposed to have this box." She looked at me and
winked. "Grace thinks we should take these
back to the kitchen, right?" I had banana
bread cheeks, so instead of talking I nodded
my head.

WHAT HAPPENED NEXT

Robert and I followed Mimi downstairs. I was
glad that we were going to the kitchen—I really needed to drink something. As soon as
Mimi stepped into the kitchen, she stopped. I
wasn't expecting that. I bumped into the back
of her.

THIS IS WHAT MIMI SAW

JAR OF PICKLES

BOOKS

STOOL

ROBERT'S LADDER TO GET
ONTO THE COUNTER

Mimi spun around and looked at Robert. Her eyes flashed mad, but she blinked the mad out, took a deep breath, and bent down to talk to him. "You have to stop doing this," said Mimi. She pointed to the stool. "It's dangerous. You could fall. Promise me you won't put all this stuff together to climb on the counter. Okay?" Mimi was using a serious voice but she wasn't yelling or sounding mad. If she had shouted, Robert would have for sure cried, but instead he just put his head down and mumbled something. I couldn't hear what he said, but Mimi nodded her head, gave him a hug, and then opened the box of crackers.

WHAT HAPPENED AFTER I HAD A BIG DRINK OF WATER

Mimi gave Robert two crackers and put the box back high on the shelf. "Crackers are his favorite," said Mimi. "Well, that and chocolate cake, but that's more of a special occasion thing. If Mom let him he would eat nothing but crackers. That's why we have to put them up so high." Mimi held the stool and looked around the kitchen. "Maybe Dad should put this in the basement," she said. I watched Mimi being busy. She was the same Mimi but different. I had never seen her be so mom-like before.

"You're good at taking care of someone," I said. "Really?" asked Mimi. "Yeah, you are," I said. "If I ever go on vacation I would totally let you watch Mr. Scruffers." "Wow. Okay,

thanks," said Mimi. She came over and gave my shoulder a little hug. "I'm sorry about you not being a flower girl," said Mimi. I thought she was finished talking, but then she said, "Maybe the other special thing you get to do will be even better. Augustine Dupre is pretty good with ideas." I smiled. It was my real smile because it was true. "Yeah, you're right," I said. "She is good with ideas."

WHAT I SAW ON THE WAY HOME

Mimi lives next door, so usually there is not much new stuff to see on my walk home. Today was different though. I noticed two new things right away.

THE TWO THINGS
1. A UPS truck parked right in front of my house.
2. Sammy Stringer walking on the road.

I noticed the UPS truck because I love the UPS truck. The UPS truck brings presents! I love presents! Lately we've been pretty lucky—the UPS truck has been coming by more often. Mom must be buying more stuff.

I noticed Sammy Stringer because he was walking in the middle of the street. The street is not a safe place to walk. I waved at Sammy but he didn't see me. He was looking at the sidewalk, and there sitting in the middle of the sidewalk was Crinkles. Sammy is not a cat lover. He has cat-phobia. I don't know if that's a real word, but for Sammy it's a real thing. He's 100 percent scared of cats.

Crinkles has Sammy-phobia. He 100 percent does not like Sammy. Ever since Sammy tried to catch him while wearing oven mitts, Crinkles hates him and hisses at him. I can't really blame him for that. Oven mitts are probably scary to a cat.

I called Crinkles over to get him off the sidewalk so Sammy could be safe, but he ignored me. Lately Crinkles has not been liking me very much either. I took a step closer and he got up and ran under the UPS truck. I know it's because of Mr. Scruffers, but it still kind of makes me sad. We used to be such good friends.

Mom says it's probably because I smell like Mr. Scruffers. I've been trying to wash my hands a lot, but so far Crinkles doesn't seem to be appreciating all my extra efforts.

WHAT SAMMY SAID

Lots of boys might be embarrassed if they knew you found out they are afraid of cats. They might try to hide their fear by saying things like "I like walking in the street" or "Sidewalks are for babies," but not Sammy. Sammy is not this kind of boy.

As soon as Crinkles was under the truck Sammy stepped onto the sidewalk. "Thanks," he shouted. "That was a close one!" He waved his arm in the air. I waved back like I understood what he was talking about. Sammy is a boy who always leaves behind more questions than answers.

Crinkles stayed under the UPS truck even after Sammy left. I was hoping the UPS man would be at our house, but he wasn't—I guess it was someone else on our street getting presents.

WHAT IS NICE ABOUT COMING HOME

I know that Mom and Dad love me, but no one says, "Oh my gosh, I'm so glad you're back! I missed you and I love you so so much!" better than Mr. Scruffers. Her welcome-back-homes are the best.

WHAT HAPPENED BEFORE DINNER

Mom and Dad were in the kitchen talking about dinner. "Let's take Mr. Scruffers for a walk around the block before dinner," said Mom. "Dad's making Sunday spaghetti." Sunday spaghetti is always one of two things. Either it's really good or . . . it's really bad. Unfortunately there is absolutely no way to tell which one it's going to be until you take your first bite. Mom calls it a mouth lottery. She tries to be nice because she says it's good for Dad to cook once in a while, but really I know she wishes the same thing as me.

HOW TO MAKE SUNDAY SPAGHETTI

Sunday spaghetti is scary. There is only one member of our family who always likes it.

GETTING READY

I put Mr. Scruffers out in the backyard while Mom and I were getting ready. It's a new plan we have because if Mr. Scruffers sees me walk toward her leash, she goes crazy with excitement and annoying barking. It's a ton better for everyone's ears to surprise her with the walk at the very last minute. When Mom was ready to go, I quietly opened the door to let

Mr. Scruffers in. Sometimes I can even fool her for longer by hiding her leash in my pocket. Usually she is waiting right outside the door, but today was different—she wasn't there. I walked outside to see what was going on.

WHAT I COULD NOT BELIEVE

What I saw outside was 100 percent surprising. Crinkles and Mr. Scruffers were both in the backyard—together. There was no barking, no hissing, and most surprising of all, no chasing! I watched Crinkles. He was walking funny—like the ground was covered in sticky syrup. He moved each paw up and down carefully, taking super slow motion steps across the lawn. The biggest surprise was Mr. Scruffers. She was sitting at the bottom of the stairs, perfectly still. Her eyes were watching Crinkles, but her body wasn't moving. It was like Crinkles's slow motion moves were hypnotizing her.

THE TRANCE BREAKER

Mom broke the trance when she opened the door and said, "Are we going or not?" All of a sudden Mr. Scruffers was like a rocket. She shot across the yard after Crinkles. I tried to get her to stop. "Walk time! Walk time! Walk time!" I shouted and jingled her leash. She stopped, looked at me, looked back at Crinkles, and then quickly ran up the stairs toward me. She likes a good cat chase, but lucky for Crinkles, she likes a good walk more.

WHY MR. SCRUFFERS LOVES WALKS

Squirrels!

DOGS LOVE US!

I KNOW. IT MAKES ME FEEL KIND OF FAMOUS.

Mom likes it when we take Mr. Scruffers for night walks. It's hard to see squirrels in the dark, so she doesn't bark or pull as much. I'm not sure if that's fair to Mr. Scruffers though. If I loved squirrels as much as she does, I'd be pretty disappointed if I didn't see any.

MY GOOD NIGHT TO MIMI

At bedtime, Mimi and I flashed our lights at each other. We try to do this every night. Mostly we do four flashes each. Sometimes if Robert is in her room I see him waving too. I'm pretty lucky to have my best friend right outside my bedroom window. I have tried to get Mr. Scruffers to wave, but she's not

crazy about me touching her feet. It makes
her growly.

IS TODAY A SCHOOL DAY?

This is the question Robert asks Mimi every
day. Mimi says he is always hoping for the answer to be no. This morning I was feeling the
exact same way as him. Mondays can be hard
that way.

Mimi and I walked to school with Max,
her next-door neighbor from the other side.
Max is Sammy's best friend, but he is not
like Sammy—he's more of a normal, regular
kind of boy. The most amaz-
ing thing about Max is that he
can do handstands and hand
walking. Not every-
one can do that. It's
pretty cool.

HANDS MOVE
FORWARD LIKE
FEET.

Mimi said Max tried to show Robert how to do it, but as soon as Max flipped upside down Robert ran screaming into the house. Sometimes little kids can be unpredictable.

WHY TODAY IS NOT A NORMAL DAY

On a normal day I would have lunch with Mimi, but today I don't get to do that. Today I have to go to the library to meet with Mr. Frank. He is here at the school doing a special project. Mr. Frank said it's helping him get more experience so he will be a better teacher. I didn't tell him this, but I think he's a really good teacher already. He is starting a comics club. When someone finds out you are good at something and they are making a club about that thing, they pretty much do whatever they can to get you to join their club.

I would be a lot happier about the comics club if Mimi was in it too. I tried to get her join, but it was useless. Mimi hates drawing. Lunch with Mimi is my favorite part of the day, so missing it was going to make everything feel upside down. Just thinking about it made me want to be like Robert and run away.

ANNOYERS

There are boys in our class who are annoying. I'm not trying to be mean—it's just true. The weird good thing that I have noticed is that even though there are more than one of them, they usually kind of take turns with their annoyingness. Not all of them act up at the same time. If they did Miss Lois's head would probably explode, and I wouldn't blame her. That would be a lot to handle.

ANNOYING BOY WHEEL

SPIN THE WHEEL

ANNOYER FOR TODAY

USED TO BE ONLY KIND OF ANNOYING, BUT NOW HE HANGS OUT WITH OWEN 1. HE HAS HAD A POWER-UP IN ANNOYINGNESS.

MAYBE THE NUMBER ONE TROUBLEMAKER

BRIAN ABER

OWEN 1

SAMMY

TREVOR

ROBERT WALTERS

ALWAYS ASKS DUMB QUESTIONS AND GETS INTO TROUBLE A LOT

LIKES TO TALK ABOUT DISGUSTING THINGS

DOES NOT PAY ATTENTION, LIKES TO DRAW ROBOTS AND AIRPLANES.

Today the annoyer was Owen 1. Miss Lois told him he had to wear shoes with shoelaces, but I guess he forgot. He must have opened and closed his Velcro shoe flaps about a hundred times this morning. Listening to him play with his shoes did not help my mood about missing lunch with Mimi one little bit.

WHAT HAPPENED AT LUNCHTIME

Mimi went off with Grace L. for lunch. I was happy about that. Grace L. is super nice. I thought I might be jealous but I wasn't, plus it turns out that there are more people in the comics club than I thought there were going to be. Mr. Frank is very popular. He's almost like a school celebrity—everybody likes being with him.

MR. FRANK'S PROJECT

Mr. Frank has this big idea that we should try to get to know our friends and families better and the way that we should do it is through comics. Here is what we have to do.

1. Pick a person.
2. Interview them and ask them what kind of games they used to play when they were young.
3. Write and draw a comic about what they say.

The best part of the whole thing is that Mr. Frank is going to take our comics and have them made into a book. It's going to be a real book with a hard cover and everything. The school library is going to get five copies so people can check them out and read them. Of course we all wanted copies for ourselves, but Mr. Frank said the books were too expensive and the school didn't have enough money for that. It seems like Mr. Harris, the principal, could maybe do a better job of deciding where to spend school money.

I KNOW WHAT THIS SCHOOL NEEDS, NEW SOAP DISPENSERS FOR THE BOYS' BATHROOM.

MOST OF THE BOYS DON'T EVEN USE SOAP.

Trevor asked if we could all have our names on the cover of the book. Mr. Frank said he wished we could, but that there probably wasn't room for them all to fit. "I'm sorry," said Mr. Frank. "The only name we can put on the cover is the name of the book." Suddenly Trevor said, "Hey, let's call the book Trevor!" I'm kind of surprised that Trevor is even in the comics club. He is not someone I would have picked, even if he can draw good planes.

Mr. Frank has lots of patience, because he just smiled at Trevor and said, "Very funny, but I already have a name. This book is going to be called *Community Comics*." Even though

Mr. Frank's name for the book is not very excellent, it's still a lot better than *Trevor*.

THE BAD THING ABOUT COMICS

Mr. Frank said that we each have to do at least five whole pages of comics, and that is because we have to make the book be one hundred pages long. As soon as he said this people started saying things like "Okay," "Sure," "No problem," "I could do twenty," "This will be easy," and "I'll hand mine in tomorrow." Of course, I did not say any of these things, and that is because I am the only one who is used to making comics. If you are used to making comics, you know one very important thing.

1. Drawing comics takes a super long time and you can for sure not make five pages of comics in one single night.

WHAT I COULD HAVE SAID

I didn't say this because I knew if I did people would start saying things like this . . .

. . . and I didn't want the comics club to be over because of me.

THE BAD THING ABOUT MR. FRANK

When Mr. Frank said, "Super! I knew you'd all be excited," I suddenly knew one other very important thing.

1. Mr. Frank does not know very much about comics.

And knowing this made me think of how things were probably going to go from **good**, which was how mostly everyone was feeling today, to **bad**, which is what the feelings would be in the next week. In the next meeting people were not going to be saying what they had said today. Instead they were going to be saying . . .

MR. FRANK, COMICS ARE TOO MUCH WORK. I LIKE TO READ THEM, BUT I DON'T WANT TO MAKE THEM.

ONLY TWO LITTLE PARTS OF THE COMIC ARE FINISHED.

WHAT I DID NOT WANT TO HAPPEN

I did not want Mr. Frank to be sad about his project not working out. But more than that, I did not want everyone to quit, and for me to be the only person left to do all one hundred comics by myself. The only good thing about doing all that comic drawing is that it would for sure keep me too busy to think about not being the flower girl at Augustine Dupre's wedding, but still, I did not want to do it.

Sometimes a big idea can suddenly pop right into your brain. This happens a lot on TV. It does not happen so much in real life, so when it does that's extra lucky.

MY BIG IDEA

WHAT IF WE FOUND ONE OF THOSE PHOTO BOOTH MACHINES?

WE COULD TAKE PICTURES INSTEAD OF DRAWING EVERYTHING.

WE COULD EVEN MAKE FACES LIKE WE WERE TALKING AND THEN ALL WE WOULD HAVE TO DO IS DRAW WORD BALLOONS AND PUT IN THE WORDS.

WHAT EVERYONE SAID ABOUT THE PHOTO BOOTH IDEA

"Yes! Yes! Yes!" Pretty much everyone in the world loves photo booths. They are fun, silly, and not even super expensive for the photos. If Mom would let me, I'd for sure get one for our house.

WHAT MR. FRANK SAID ABOUT THE PHOTO BOOTH IDEA

Right away I could tell that Mr. Frank liked the idea. "I like the idea," said Mr. Frank. "But I think those photo booth machines are pretty expensive. We don't have enough money for that. But maybe we could take regular photos and make them look like photo booth photos. Or maybe you could draw pretend photos. Wait . . ."

Mr. Frank held his finger in the air. He stopped talking. We all watched his brain work. He closed his eyes—four or five seconds later they suddenly opened. "I got it!" shouted Mr. Frank. Grace F. screamed and dropped her pencil. She was standing right next to Mr. Frank, and she was not expecting him to shout. In fact, none of us was. It was very exciting.

MR. FRANK'S NEW PROJECT

1. Call the book *Community Comics: The Photo Booth Book.*
2. Pick a person.
3. Interview them and ask them what kind of games they used to play when they were young.
4. Use only four squares to tell the story.

THIS IS WHAT EACH
PAGE WILL LOOK LIKE

THIS IS WHAT WE CAN USE TO TELL ABOUT OUR INTERVIEW

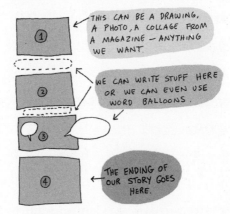

Everyone was in love with Mr. Frank's new idea. It was a great idea, and lots better than the original one.

THE TWO REASONS WHY I WAS SUPER HAPPY

1. I didn't say anything about it, but I was feeling that my brain had worked in exactly the same way that Augustine

Dupre's brain does. My brain gave Mr. Frank a new idea, and he didn't even know I had done it. Too bad I couldn't give his brain the idea to make Miss Lois let us watch a movie all afternoon. For sure I'd have to practice more before I was good enough to do that kind of brain control.

2. Mr. Frank was letting us tell our interview stories without having to make drawings. That meant one thing—maybe I could get Mimi to be in the club too!

WHAT MR. FRANK SAID BEFORE WE LEFT AND AFTER MAX SPILLED HIS SOUP ON THE LIBRARY CARPET

At first he said, "OH, NO!" Then when he was on the carpet with all the paper towels he said, "From now on please don't bring soup or anything in a thermos for lunch on comics club day. Bring a sandwich! See you next week. And have fun with those interviews."

I was just about to step out of the library when Mr. Frank called my name. I thought he might be needing me to get him some more paper towels for the soup, but instead he said, "Thanks, Grace, for all your help. I appreciate it!" I was surprised. I guess I'm not as good at secret mind control as Augustine Dupre is. If you are good at it the person whose mind you controlled doesn't even know you did anything. I nodded my head and smiled, but I don't think he saw me. He was pretty busy scooping up noodles.

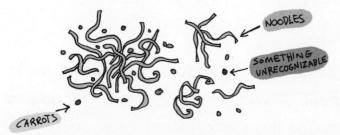

NOODLES

SOMETHING UNRECOGNIZABLE

CARROTS

WHAT CAN MAKE YOUR DAY GO FROM GOOD TO EXCELLENT

The rest of the day was pretty ordinary, and somehow, even though Owen 1 was still messing with his shoes, it didn't bug me as much.

On the way home I told Mimi all about the comics project. I tried to sound super excited so that she would want to do it too. After about the millionth time of promising her, "There's no drawing at all! You don't have to draw!" she finally said yes. "Okay, I'll try it," said Mimi. "But if I don't like it, I get to leave." "You'll stay," I said, and that was because I knew one thing. Mr. Frank is the nicest teacher in the world. Mimi would be like me. She would want to help him.

WHAT I SAW WHEN I GOT HOME

The UPS truck was parked outside my house again. I wasn't expecting anything, but still maybe there was a surprise for me. I said a quick goodbye to Mimi and ran inside. Mr. Scruffers instantly attacked me. It's not easy to take off your shoes and hang up your coat when there is a dog jumping on you and barking like crazy. Finally I just picked her up. She always calms down when I hold her. Good thing she's pretty small.

BIG DOG VERSUS MR. SCRUFFERS

Mom was in the kitchen. "Mom, did we get any packages? A present for me? The UPS truck is outside." Mom shook her head and said, "The only one in this house who is getting lots of presents is Augustine Dupre. She's the one getting married." I thought about this for a second. "Does she get to open them before the wedding?" I asked. Mom looked up. I knew she was trying to read my mind, so I just smiled. "I think so," said Mom. "Why are you . . . ?" Before she could say anything else I dropped Mr. Scruffers on the floor and ran down to the basement. If there is one thing I love, it's opening presents! Maybe Augustine Dupre needed some help. Lucky for her, I happen to be an excellent present opener.

PRESENT OPENER SKILLS

1. DO NOT TAKE A LONG TIME TO RIP THE WRAPPING PAPER OFF THE PRESENT.

2. DO NOT TEAR UP THE PRESENT BOX BY MISTAKE.

3. SAY NICE THINGS ABOUT THE PRESENT, EVEN IF YOU DON'T REALLY LIKE IT.

WHAT I WAS 100 PERCENT SURPRISED ABOUT

Augustine Dupre was not alone. When she answered the door, there standing right next to her was the UPS man. At first I mostly noticed his brown uniform, but then I looked up at his face. "AHHHHH!" I screamed. "It's you!" I pointed, and then covered my mouth. I couldn't speak. Nobody could. We just stood there, all three of us, with surprised faces.

WHAT HAPPENED NEXT

Luke was the first one to go back to normal. He smiled—it was the smile from the photo booth photo. "Are you okay?" he asked. "I didn't mean to scare you." My brain was thinking of a million things, but somehow my mouth was still able to work. "Yeah, I'm okay . . . uh. Hi," I said. And then I put my hand up for a mini-wave.

Augustine Dupre was the next person to speak. "Grace, would you like to come in? I have some lemonade and cake, or cookies or croissants?" I nodded yes and walked straight to the kitchen table and sat down. It was nice to get off my legs. They were feeling a little wobbly.

WHAT HAPPENED FOR THE REST OF THE VISIT

Augustine Dupre and Luke were both super nice to me. It was weird to see them together without Luke just delivering a package and then leaving. Of course now that I was sitting at the table with him, I was a little embarrassed that I had not remembered who he was.

We ate Augustine Dupre's homemade croissants, drank lemonade, and talked about the wedding. Augustine Dupre and Luke did most of the talking. I was just happy to listen, because my brain was pretty busy trying to get used to everything I was now knowing.

They told me their love story of how they met.

They told me they were getting married in two weeks because that's when Luke's family was going to be visiting from France.

AUGUSTINE DUPRE'S HOMEMADE CROISSANT.

THEY HAVE NEVER BEEN HERE BEFORE, SO OUR WEDDING WILL MAKE THE VISIT EXTRA SPECIAL.

They told me that they were thinking about something special for me to do at the wedding. That part wasn't figured out yet, but it was nice that they were still thinking about it.

And then right before it was time for me to go, Augustine Dupre showed me a few of the presents she was extra excited about. At first I was disappointed that they were already opened, but when I saw what they were I was a lot less disappointed about that part.

SPECIAL BIG BOWL FOR SOUP

NAPKINS WITH BIRDS ON THEM.

ANTIQUE SALAD DRESSING HOLDER

Birthday presents are definitely more exciting than wedding presents. It wouldn't have been very exciting to open any of these!

THE BIG QUESTION I ASKED AUGUSTINE DUPRE WHEN SHE WALKED ME TO THE DOOR

"Are you moving away?"

THE ANSWER

Augustine put her hand on my shoulder and said, "We can't stay here forever, but for now we have no plans to move. Luke likes it here too." It was the best answer I could hope for. If Crinkles understood English he would have been happy too. The love of his life was not going to be moving away.

THE REST OF MY NIGHT

Nothing super exciting happened. I had

dinner, did my homework, and went to bed without even asking to stay up ten extra minutes. And even though there was no way she could understand me, I told Mr. Scruffers all about my visit with Augustine Dupre. Sometimes it feels good to just say stuff out loud.

TUESDAY

The most important thing that happened all day happened the minute I met Mimi outside for our walk to school. "Guess what?" I said. "What?" asked Mimi. "You'll never guess. Not in a million years!" I said. "Well, then tell me!" said Mimi. She was wearing her impatient face, the one that means *I don't want to guess anymore!* I looked at her, took a big breath, and said, "Guess who Augustine Dupre is going to marry? It's the UPS man!"

WHAT MIMI'S FACE SAID

BIG SURPRISED EYES.

OPEN SURPRISED MOUTH

WHAT MIMI'S MOUTH SAID

"OHMYGOSHICAN'TBELIEVEITAREYOUKI
DDINGWOWTHAT'SSOCRAZYICAN'TBELI
EVEITTHEUPSMANISLUKE? WOW!!!"

It's a good thing I know Mimi or I would have never been able to understand what she was saying, and that is because she said it all without stopping to take even one single breath.

WHAT WE DID THE REST OF THE DAY

Mimi and I pretty much spent the whole rest of the day doing schoolwork and talking about Augustine Dupre. Mimi had one big question. I didn't know the answer, but I was really hoping the answer was no.

Right when school ended, Grace F. came up to me to show me her comic for Mr. Frank. It is no surprise she is in the comics club, because she's a very good artist. Seeing her comic made me excited to work more on mine. "I'm doing one as soon as I get home," I promised. "Oh, good," she said. "I'm going to do another one too." I wasn't the only one who wanted to make Mr. Frank happy. That was nice to see.

WHAT WAS NOT IN FRONT OF MY HOUSE

The UPS truck, and this was a surprise. Now that I knew who Luke was, I was suddenly understanding why there was always a UPS truck parked on our street. Well, not always, but a lot. I had even seen Luke knocking on Augustine Dupre's door, but I just always thought he was delivering a package. I never thought he was staying and visiting. That's what's weird about life—you have to pay attention or you miss stuff.

SOMETIMES EVEN IF YOU KNOW SOMEONE REALLY GOOD, THEY CAN STILL SURPRISE YOU

Since Mom was the only one home, I had to choose her as my interview person. "What kind of cool games did you play when you were a kid?" I asked. I was expecting her to say something like tag or hide-and-seek, but she didn't. What she said was a lot more interesting. It was the kind of thing that made me want to march right upstairs to my room and draw. And that's exactly what I did, after a snack and fifteen minutes of playing chase with Mr. Scruffers.

When I get working on a drawing, I don't like to stop until I am done. Lucky for me, I finished before bedtime.

MOM'S GAME
KITTY BOWLING

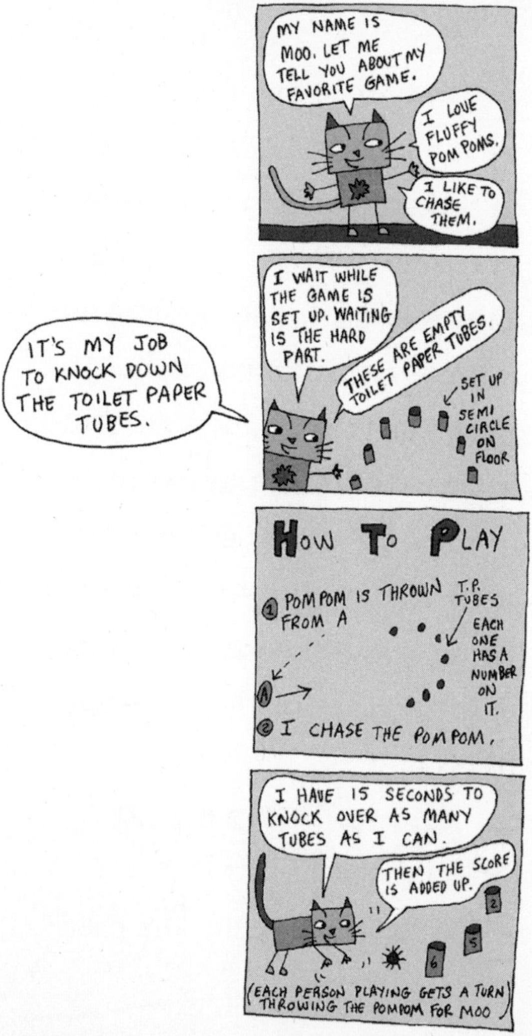

WEDNESDAY

I wouldn't let Mimi see my comic until lunchtime. I was dying to show it to her, but I wanted to save it for the comics club—that way her first day there would be even more interesting.

When you are waiting for something to happen and you are excited about it, the waiting time part always goes by really slow. This happened today. The whole morning seemed to take six hours to go by instead of three like normal. The only good thing was that Owen 1 was wearing lace-up shoes. I noticed because when I dropped my pencil I saw him twisting his laces around his fingers.

THE COMICS CLUB

Mr. Frank could hardly stop smiling and used

lots of words like *amazing, fantastic, beautiful, creative,* and *wonderful.* Everyone had worked on their comic, which was a big surprise. Not everyone was finished, but still they had all tried. Mr. Frank was right to feel happy. Miss Lois can't get this much stuff done in her class unless she threatens to put people's names on the board.

MY FAVORITE PROJECT

Max's project was my favorite because it was super creative and unusual. Max said his mom wouldn't let him take her photo, so instead, he made her face out of Legos. He took photos of the Lego face, printed them out, and used them for the project. Of course his mom looks a ton different in real life, but I like her Lego look too.

CAMEL AND PENGUIN

MAX'S PROJECT →

FIRST YOU NEED SOMETHING TO HIDE. WE USED TO HIDE A RED BALL WE HAD.

ONE PERSON HIDES THE BALL.

EVERYONE ELSE HAS TO TRY AND FIND THE BALL. IF YOU GET CLOSE THE HIDER YELLS "CAMEL."

IF YOU ARE FAR AWAY THE HIDER YELLS "PENGUIN." THE FIRST PERSON TO FIND THE BALL IS THE WINNER.

THE BEST PART WAS THE END. EVERYONE WOULD BE RUNNING AROUND LIKE CRAZY.

IT WAS FUN TO HIDE THE BALL.

WHAT MIMI LOOKED LIKE THE WHOLE TIME

I COULD DO THIS.

Mr. Frank asked for all the finished comics. He said he was going to start a school gallery on one of the walls in the library—that way other kids would see them and maybe want to make some too. I think he was like me, suddenly knowing that our little group was not going to have such an easy time making a hundred comics.

Fifty kids making two comics each was probably going to be easier than fifteen kids making five or six comics each.

My comic looked good on the wall. "I like

it," said Mimi. She was standing next to me. "It makes me want to do one too!" "I knew you would," I said. I tried not to sound too excited. For some reason having Mimi do this comic thing with me was sort of important. I don't know why.

It was like eating something delicious and saying to your friend, "Hey, try this—it's great." And then both of you are eating it and loving it together.

YOU'RE RIGHT, THIS IS AMAZING.

I DON'T KNOW WHY, BUT HAVING YOU LIKE IT TOO MAKES IT TASTE MORE DELICIOUS.

THE ONE BAD THING ABOUT HAVING THE COMICS ON THE WALL FOR EVERYONE TO SEE

I was secretly hoping Sammy Stringer would not see the comics and want to make one.

I like Sammy, but he has a lot of disgusting ideas. He makes things with garbage and chewed-up gum. I do not want my comic, which I love, to be anywhere near one of his creations. I would feel a whole lot better if all Sammy's projects came to school in zippered plastic bags—maybe even taped shut to be extra safe.

EXTRA TAPE

SAMMY'S COMIC MADE OUT OF SOMETHING STRANGE

WALKING HOME WITH MAX, SAMMY, AND MIMI

On the way home from school Mimi and I told Max and Sammy all about the UPS man and Augustine Dupre. They were not as excited as we were. Sammy's one big question was "Does she get to ride in the back of the UPS truck?" I looked at Sammy and shook my head. Why would Augustine Dupre even want to ride in the back of a truck with a bunch of boxes?

After that I did not mention the part about me not being the flower girl. I had a big feeling that Sammy and Max would care even less about that.

WHAT SAMMY WOULD SAY

WHY WOULD YOU WANT TO THROW DUMB FLOWERS?

WHY CAN'T YOU THROW SOMETHING GOOD LIKE CANDY OR MONEY?

When we got to my house Max wanted to come in and see Mr. Scruffers. He has this big idea that he can train her to do a backflip. He saw a dog do one on TV and has been dying to try it. Sammy was definitely not filled with joy about that idea. He is not an animal person. Instead of everyone coming in, I said I would go in, get Mr. Scruffers, and bring her out. I was pretty sure Mom would like that idea better. Mimi ran to her house to get Robert. It was nice of her to think about him. Robert would be crazy excited to see Mr. Scruffers do a backflip.

THE BACKFLIP THAT NEVER HAPPENED

Teaching a dog to do a backflip is not as easy as Max thought it was. I brought out some dog treats for him to use but Mr. Scruffers wasn't one bit interested. She completely ignored Max, the treats, and even me. Instead she had laser eyes for Robert and his crackers.

WHAT WAS IMPOSSIBLE

It was impossible to get Robert to give up any of his crackers. Mimi tried, Max tried, and even I tried. You might think that saying, "Robert, give me a cracker and I'll make Mr. Scruffers do a backflip" would get you a cracker. But if you thought that, you would be wrong.

Max even had the good idea of asking Mimi to go inside and get the cracker box, but he made one big mistake. He said his idea out loud in front of Robert. Robert didn't want anyone to touch any of the crackers! Even the ones inside.

WHAT WOULD BE A GOOD IDEA

For the people who make dog treats to make them taste more like Robert's favorite crackers.

WHAT SAMMY SAID

Sammy did not have much to say about the whole backflip thing except for asking Max, "Can we go?" every couple of minutes. I was surprised when he suddenly said, "Why is the cat walking in slow motion?" We all turned and looked to where Sammy was pointing. There was Crinkles, doing his sticky-paw walking. Mr. Scruffers was watching too. She had one eye on Robert and one eye on Crinkles, but she didn't move or make a sound. "How do you make her do that?" asked Mimi. "Not bark or go after Crinkles?" "I'm not doing anything," I said. "She just does it."

Crinkles was next to the bushes at the far side of the yard. I'm sure that Sammy was happy that he was walking away from us instead of toward us. "He's walking like one of those horses," said Max. "You know, the kind that do the foot-thing in parades." "Yeah, fancy walking," said Mimi. "Like a . . . uh." She looked at me and shrugged her shoulders. Just because you want to say something doesn't mean you can always find the right word. I shrugged my shoulders back at her, and when we looked back at the bushes Crinkles was gone.

"Cats are creepy," said Sammy. "Too bad they don't walk slow like that all the time."

IF CATS ARE SLOW YOU CAN SEE THEM COMING FROM FAR AWAY.

WHAT BROKE THE SPELL

As soon as Robert popped the last crumb of cracker into his mouth, Mr. Scruffers jumped up and began sniffing around. She was back to her old self. She barked a few times at the bushes, just in case Crinkles was hiding in there. "Can we go?" asked Sammy for the millionth time. Max looked around, nodded, and they walked off to Max's house. Mimi said she had to take Robert home too. He was not excited to leave. Mimi had to do some dragging. I listened to them talk as they crossed the yard. It was cute.

Robert: What about the backflip?

Mimi: Mr. Scruffers didn't want to do it.

Robert: Why?

Mimi: Well, because maybe she didn't feel like it.

Robert: Like I didn't feel like giving her a cracker.

Mimi: Exactly!

Robert: Mr. Scruffers is like me. We know what we don't like.

WHAT MOM SAID

At dinner I told Mom and Dad about Mr. Scruffers and the backflip that never happened. Dad said he wasn't surprised that it hadn't worked out—a backflip is a complicated trick. Mom said, "It's probably easier to teach her a trick that uses something she already knows how to do. Like sit for a treat." I looked down at Mr. Scruffers. She was sitting next to my chair watching me eat. "Yeah, I guess that's her trick," I said. "And she's excellent at it, especially if it's for a cracker!"

WHAT IS TRUE

Right before bed I gave Mr. Scruffers some special hugs. "I love you even if you can't do amazing tricks," I said. She probably couldn't understand me, but she liked the hugs and extra petting. That part I could tell.

HER HEAD ON
MY PILLOW. →

MY LIFE
IS GOOD.

THURSDAY

Mimi and I talked wedding-talk all the way to school. It's sad, but Mimi is not invited to come. Mom says Augustine Dupre is having a super-small wedding of only thirty-two people. I don't know why she can't have thirty-three people and invite Mimi, but Mom says I'm not allowed to ask. I'm surprised, but Mimi is not sad. She said she might watch it from my bedroom window if Mom says it's okay.

Mimi and I talked about

- my special job—I still don't know what it is going to be.

- my new dress—I get to have one even though I'm not the flower girl.
- wedding presents—which are surprisingly boring and not good.

SCALE OF WEDDING GOODNESS

WHAT HAPPENED AT SCHOOL

Sometimes I feel like there are two Miss Loises. The old Miss Lois, who was the Miss Lois we got at the start of the year, and the new Miss Lois, the one we have now. The new

Miss Lois looks exactly the same as the old Miss Lois, but she is a lot more fun. She got that way because of Mr. Frank.

Today we got to play charades all morning. We have been learning facts about the different states—there's a lot to remember. Miss Lois said she had a big plan about how to help us. She divided the class into two teams and gave each team some cards. The cards were charade cards and had facts to act out about each state. She had the good idea to let us make sounds too, which helped a lot with the guessing. Our team lost, but I don't care. It was 100 percent more fun than doing math problems. I'm pretty sure I'll never forget the state bird

SUNNI BEING A MOCKINGBIRD, WHICH IS THE STATE BIRD OF TEXAS.

CAW, CAW, TWEET, TWEET. SKREECH, SKREECH.

NO ONE GUESSED HERS, BUT IT WAS FUN TO WATCH.

of Texas. All I have to do is think of Sunni and I'll remember.

LUNCHTIME

There is one good thing about not having a brother or a sister and that is, you never get the wrong lunch. I was sitting across from Marta today. Poor Marta! She got her sister's lunch. I don't know how anyone could like pickled herring, but I guess her sister does. Marta was pretty upset!

OH NO! THIS IS POLLY'S LUNCH!

I HATE PICKLED HERRING.

FISH PRETENDING TO BE A PICKLE.

WHAT HAPPENED IN THE AFTERNOON

We had a regular school afternoon. The morning part was much better.

WHAT HAPPENED ON THE WAY HOME

Mimi told me the story about a game her dad played when he was a kid. I was pretty surprised to hear it, because her dad as a grown-up seems super nice and kind. The game was called Let's Find Rory. When Mimi's dad was little, Rory was a super-annoying kid that lived next door to him. The game was for Rory to hide and then all the kids would try to find him, only the truth was, they never tried to find him. They just pretended they were trying. Mimi's dad said it was a good way to get rid of Rory for a couple of hours. I guess all the kids were super good actors, because the Rory kid never figured it out. He just always thought he was an amazing hider. Mimi's dad said everyone loved that game—especially Rory.

Mimi said she was going to do her comic about the Rory game. As soon as we got home Mimi ran inside. She sure was excited to get started on her comic. I was secretly wondering if she was going to sew something. Mimi is crazy for sewing things.

MOM'S BIG BAD PRESENT

After Mr. Scruffers had barked about three hundred times and jumped on me for about ten minutes, I was finally able to get my stuff out of my backpack and put it away like Mom likes. Mom was sitting at the counter, looking at her computer. "Grace, come help," she said. "I can't decide. Which of these do you think Augustine Dupre would like better?" I looked over her shoulder. Mom was looking at two silver bowls. They looked almost the same. "I know she wants a silver bowl, but I'm just not sure which one to get. Which one do you like?" I looked again. They were both not exciting. "I don't know, Mom. Why are you buying her a bowl?" Mom looked up and smiled. "It's a wedding present . . . from all of us."

WHAT I SAID TO MOM

"A bowl? That's our present? That's the worst present ever! She doesn't want a bowl! You have to give her something good! Something important! NOT A STUPID DUMB BORING BOWL!"

WHAT MOM SAID

"GRACE STEWART! I will not tolerate that tone of voice from you! For your information, Augustine Dupre told me she wanted a silver bowl, so that means she will like getting a silver bowl, and these happen to be very expensive, nice silver bowls that I am sure she would be thrilled to own! If you do not like the gift we are giving her as a family, then you are welcome to buy your own gift! Now go upstairs and do not come down unless it's to apologize." Mom turned around and with a mad finger tapped her keyboard. From where I was standing with my head down I could see the little arrow on her computer. It was right on the word *buy*.

I turned around and stomped upstairs. I was never apologizing. I was just going to live in my room forever!

THE WORLD'S WORST PRESENT

THINGS THAT ARE GOOD
ABOUT THIS BOWL.

1 -
2 -
3 -
4 -

NOTHING!!!

WHAT IS NOT EASY

I counted my money. I had $13.57. It's probably not easy to buy a great wedding present for under $20.00.

WHAT I SHOULD NOT HAVE DONE

I looked at my bookshelf. It was filled with comic books—I had lots of thoughts in my head.

I had read them all, and now most of my money was gone.

WHAT I SAID TO MR. SCRUFFERS

"Mr. Scruffers, this is the worst day ever!" I tried to be cozy with her on the bed, but she squirmed away and ran over to the window. It was her superpower working, because there was Crinkles, carefully walking across the grass—like he was in a parade, like he was on stage, like he was walking down an aisle. And that's when I thought of it . . . FLOWER CAT!

THE BEST WEDDING PRESENT THAT I EVER THOUGHT OF IN MY WHOLE ENTIRE LIFE THAT AUGUSTINE DUPRE IS GOING TO 100 PERCENT LOVE AND REMEMBER FOREVER

I am going to train Crinkles to walk down the aisle in Augustine Dupre's wedding!

WHAT I DID NEXT

I ran downstairs to set the table for dinner and apologize to Mom. At first she still seemed kind of mad, but after I said, "I really think a silver bowl would look nice with Augustine Dupre's fancy French dishes," she seemed better. "And," said Mom, "if you want to do something special you could make the card to go with it. You're so good at drawing." "Sure!" I said. "Plus I might do something else too." Mom smiled. "I'm glad you're happy again." "Me too!" I said.

FRIDAY

What I know about training a cat:

Nothing.

What I know about how a wedding works.

Nothing.

Mimi and I were definitely going to have to do some research at the library at school.

I waited outside on the path for Mimi. I could tell that she was about to come outside because Robert was at her door opening it and closing it—plus he had pushed her back-pack outside. I couldn't tell if he was mad or just trying to help her get out of the house fast.

Finally Mimi came bursting out the door. "Run," she whispered. "Bye!" she shouted. She waved behind her and raced off down the street ahead of me. I followed as fast as I could. Mimi can run fast when she wants to.

"Why are we running?" I gasped. I was out of breath and not super happy.

MIMI'S BIG EXPLANATION

Mimi's explanation took up the whole walk to school. I didn't get a turn to talk and tell her about Flower Cat. As soon as we got to school, the bell rang and there was no more time for chatting. The whole thing made me feel grumpier than I wanted to be.

...SO I TOLD MOM THAT I DIDN'T GIVE HIM THE CRACKERS, AND SHE SAID...

THIS STORY IS NEVER GOING TO END.

Question: Why was Mimi running?
Answer: So Robert couldn't follow her.

Just because a story is long, does not mean it is interesting.

WHAT I COULD HARDLY WAIT FOR

LUNCHTIME!

I wasn't mad anymore, and I couldn't wait to tell Mimi about Flower Cat! Even though Mimi is allergic to cats, I knew she was for sure going to love the idea.

WHAT MIMI LOVED

FLOWER CAT!!!!

She especially loved the drawing I made. "That would look great on a T-shirt," said Mimi. "I'd definitely wear that." "Me too," I said, because she was right. It was super cute!

WHAT I NOW KNOW ABOUT TRAINING CATS

Mimi and I used all our library time to do cat and wedding research. We found out one big thing about cat training. It is one hundred times easier to train a dog than to train a cat. Cats are not at all like dogs!

TRICKS	SIT	STAY	ROLL OVER	SHAKE
DOG	YES	YES	YES	YES
CAT	NO	NO	NO	NO

Cat brains do not like to learn new tricks.

I DO NOT LIKE TO BE TOLD WHAT TO DO.

EARS THAT PRETEND NOT TO HEAR YOU WHEN YOU CALL ITS NAME.

WHAT I NOW KNOW ABOUT WEDDINGS

BRIDE

WEARS A BEAUTIFUL DRESS →

GROOM

WEARS A NICE SUIT AND HOPEFULLY NOT HIS UPS UNIFORM.

BRIDE AND GROOM STAND HERE.

THEY LOOK AT THIS PERSON. (THIS PERSON MARRIES THEM.)

THE ACTUAL GETTING-MARRIED PART HAPPENS HERE.

GUESTS GUESTS
GUESTS GUESTS
GUESTS GUESTS
GUESTS GUESTS

WHERE THE GUESTS SIT

WEDDING AISLE TO WALK DOWN

When the wedding starts the bride and the groom do NOT walk down the aisle first. Here is the list of who gets to walk down the aisle first.

1. The bridesmaids and the groomsmen (I don't know if Augustine Dupre is having any of these).
2. The flower girl. (All by herself!)
3. The bride with her father. (Does Augustine Dupre have a father?)

Then the getting-married part starts.

The whole time the bride and the groom are getting married you can only see their backs, not their faces. They DO NOT look down the aisle and smile at everyone who came to watch them while they are doing the getting-married part.

WHAT WAS NOT GOOD NEWS

Everything we found out!

WHAT IS REALLY HARD TO DO

Give up on an idea when you really love it

and have even made a drawing about it that you would 100 percent wear on a T-shirt.

WHAT I WANTED TO HAPPEN AT AUGUSTINE DUPRE'S WEDDING

I wanted Augustine Dupre to be standing at the top part of the aisle and then turn around and look back and see Crinkles doing his slow paw walking all the way up to her. If Augustine Dupre saw this, she would for sure never forget her wedding. It would be the best present ever!

HER HEART IS FILLED WITH LOVE.

CRINKLES WALKING UP THE AISLE ALL THE WAY TO AUGUSTINE DUPRE.

WHAT MIMI SAID

Mimi looked at me—she was wearing her sad eyes. I could tell she was feeling empathy feelings for me. "It was a great idea," she said. "Don't be sad about not doing it." I looked back at her and smiled. "Who says we can't do it?" I asked. I held my finger up. "Flower Cat has to happen!" "How?" asked Mimi. I shrugged my shoul- ders. "I don't know that part yet. I have to think first." Mimi smiled. "You're a good think- er," she said. "Think, Grace. Think!"

THIS ISN'T EASY.

BRAIN TRYING TO THINK.

WHAT HAPPENED AFTER SCHOOL

Max and Sammy walked home with us again. Sammy seemed grumpy. I heard him whispering to Max. "Do we have to pssst psst pssst psst dog thing?" "What's the dog thing?" I asked. Max stuck his hand into his backpack and pulled out a plastic bag. "Crackers!" he said "For the backflip. Can we do it?" For some reason I wasn't excited about Mr. Scruffers doing backflips anymore. Maybe it was what Dad had said, because now, somehow, it just didn't seem fair to Mr. Scruffers.

SOMETIMES YOU HAVE TO DO STUFF THAT IS NOT EASY

When the not-easy thing is saying no to a friend, you have to choose the best words you can so their feelings don't get hurt.

BAD CHOICE OF WORDS

"I don't want you to train MY DOG to do a backflip!"

GOOD CHOICE OF WORDS

"I'm sorry, Max, but I don't think it's a good idea to have Mr. Scruffers do a backflip. She might get hurt, and it's not really a natural thing for her to do."

WHAT CAN HAPPEN EVEN IF YOU USE THE GOOD WORDS

Your friend can still get mad. Max shook the plastic bag. "I brought these from home and everything! No fair! You wanted to do it before!" He looked at me to see if I would change my mind, but I shook my head no. "Fine!" he said. He turned and stomped off. Sammy was the only one who suddenly seemed happy. "Hey Max!" he shouted. "Can I have the crackers if you aren't going to use them?" Max threw the bag onto the ground and kept walking. "Score!" shouted Sammy.

He ran to the bag, opened it, and started eating. He looked back at us and waved. He shouted something else but we couldn't tell what it was. It's not easy to understand someone with a mouth full of crackers.

WHAT MIMI AND I SAID TO EACH OTHER AT THE EXACT SAME TIME

And it wasn't an I'm-so-excited-I-can't-believe-that-amazing-thing-just-happened wow.

It was more of a that-sure-was-not-what-I-was-expecting wow.

WHAT MOM SAID WHEN I GOT INSIDE

"Grace, look what Luke brought." She was holding a big brown box. "Luke bought me a present?" I couldn't believe it. "Oh," said Mom, and she laughed. "No, I bought the present. Luke brought the package because—" I interrupted her: "He's the UPS man! Very funny, Mom, and also very confusing." Mom laughed again and shook the box. "Open it up!" she said. "Now. Here." She handed me the box. I dropped my coat on the floor.

WHAT I SAID WHEN I OPENED THE BOX

"Oh my gosh, Mom! It's amazing!" It was the most beautiful silver dress I had ever seen, and there were shoes to go with it too. It was perfect—a perfect wedding outfit. "Can I try it on?" I asked. "Now?" "Of course!" said Mom. I could hear Mr. Scruffers barking in the backyard. "Leave her outside," said Mom. "We'll let her in later. I don't want her jumping all over your new dress. Now go upstairs and model for me."

MY FAVORITE THING ABOUT THE NEW OUTFIT

The dress was amazing, but my most favorite thing of all was the new shoes, and the clicking noises they made each time I took a step. They sounded just like Mom's fancy shoes. Mom's shoes were for sure higher, but still these were great.

"Oh, Grace!" said Mom. "You look so grown up!" I smiled. "Watch," I said. I started a fancy twirl but something went wrong. All of a sudden my feet slipped. I flapped my arms but the air couldn't hold me. "AHH-HHH!" FLUMP! I landed in a heap on the bed. "I'm okay," I whimpered. I looked over at Mom and saw her covering her mouth, she was trying not to laugh. "Maybe we should practice walking before spinning," she said. I looked at my feet. "Stupid awesome shoes!" I said. And then I smiled, "I love them!"

HEELS!

THE PLAN FOR SUNDAY

Augustine Dupre was going to have a practice wedding. Mom said it's a normal thing to do, so that everyone can know what they are supposed to do on the real wedding day. Mom said practice weddings are usually closer to the real wedding, but Sunday was the only day everyone in Augustine Dupre's wedding could get together. I wanted to wear my new dress but Mom said I had to save it for the real wedding. She did not say the same thing about the new shoes. For those she said, "Practice makes perfect!"

QUIET TO CRAZY

The next morning Mimi and Robert came over right when we were cleaning up breakfast stuff. Mimi said she was bringing Robert over to play with Mr. Scruffers. Mimi's mom likes him to get exercise. Mimi said Robert is like a dog—he needs running-around time or else he gets annoying and loud in the house. Her big idea was for Robert to get tired out by chasing Mr. Scruffers in my backyard. It was a good idea.

Robert is cute. He likes to pretend he and Mr. Scruffers are best friends. I told Mimi about my fancy shoes. She said she couldn't wait to see them. Just when we were going to call Robert and Mr. Scruffers inside, Robert suddenly yelled, "Squirrel!" and pointed to a branch way up in the tree. Mr. Scruffers went crazy! "I'm helping find squirrels," yelled Robert, and then he started barking too.

DUM DE DUM.

WHAT MOM SAID

Two minutes later Mom stuck her head out the door. "What's going on out here?" she shouted. "What's wrong with the dog?" It's hard not to notice Mr. Scruffers when she is going crazy. "Squirrel!" I shouted, and I pointed at the tree. "Well go pick her up and bring her inside," said Mom. "All that noise must be driving the neighbors crazy, and it's not helping that Robert's out there barking with her!" When I went to get Mr. Scruffers, I looked up at the squirrel. He didn't seem one bit scared!

WHY ROBERT WAS SUPER HAPPY

It only took about a minute to get everyone in the house. Mr. Scruffers always calms down the minute you pick her up. Robert was still excited and was chatting like crazy. "We're a dog team," said Robert. He pointed to Mr. Scruffers. "We fight squirrels." "Good job," I said. "Here, these are for you." I dumped a handful of crackers onto a plate. "Stay here and eat. Mimi and I will be right back." Robert nodded his head—his mouth was already full. Mr. Scruffers sat down right next to Robert's chair so she could watch every bite. "He's okay. Let's go," said Mimi. "I want to see those shoes!"

WHAT MIMI SAID ABOUT MY SHOES

She loved them. I knew she would. I let her try them on, even though my feet are bigger than hers. "These are hard to walk in," said Mimi. "You're right," I said. "They're pretty tricky shoes."

PRETTY AND TRICKY

When we came back downstairs, Robert wasn't sitting at the table anymore.

"Robert! Where are you?" shouted Mimi. "Woof," said someone. Mimi and I followed the woof to the TV room. Robert was sitting in Mr. Scruffers's bed and Mr. Scruffers was sitting on the sofa. "Oh, Robert," said Mimi. "You know you're not a real dog, right?" "Woof," said Robert. "Paw," said Mimi. Robert held up his hand for her to shake. Mimi looked at me and smiled. "He's easy to train," she said. "Plus he already knew how to do that because Mom makes him show her his hands before dinner, to check that they are clean." "Woof," said Robert. "Yes, you're a good dog," said Mimi.

After Mimi and Robert left, I had one big thought. I sure wish getting Crinkles to do tricks was as easy as getting Robert to do tricks.

WHAT I KNOW

Teaching a cat a new trick is hard to do, maybe even impossible, so instead I decided to make a list of things that Crinkles already knew how to do. Maybe that would help.

WHAT CRINKLES CAN DO

- Walk really slowly across our lawn—especially if Mr. Scruffers is watching him.
- Hiss at Sammy and not go near him.
- Not come when I call him.
- Do anything to be with Augustine Dupre.
- Wear a collar with his name on it.
- Lick a tuna fish can clean.
- Jump into and then sit in any kind of empty box.

This was not a big list. Crinkles is not super talented. But still, maybe that was okay. Maybe he could do what I needed him to do anyway.

WHAT IS THE MOST IMPORTANT THING ON THE LIST

WHAT CAN MAKE MR. SCRUFFERS STAY IN ONE PLACE AND NOT MOVE

There is only one thing that makes Mr. Scruffers be the best-behaved dog in the whole world, and that thing is Robert eating crackers. When she watches Robert eat, Mr.

Scruffers sits as still as a statue—only her eyes move.

MY PLAN SO FAR

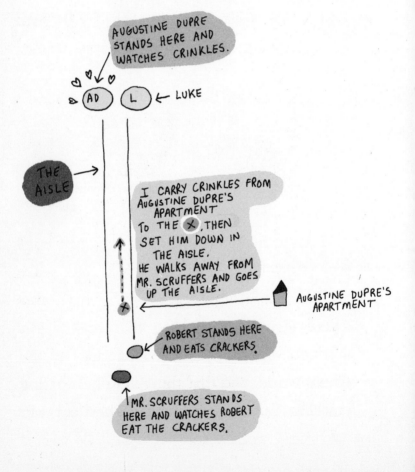

AUGUSTINE DUPRE STANDS HERE AND WATCHES CRINKLES.

(AD) (L) ← LUKE

THE AISLE →

I CARRY CRINKLES FROM AUGUSTINE DUPRE'S APARTMENT TO THE ⊗ ,THEN SET HIM DOWN IN THE AISLE. HE WALKS AWAY FROM MR. SCRUFFERS AND GOES UP THE AISLE.

AUGUSTINE DUPRE'S APARTMENT

ROBERT STANDS HERE AND EATS CRACKERS.

↑MR. SCRUFFERS STANDS HERE AND WATCHES ROBERT EAT THE CRACKERS.

CAN YOU BE A FLOWER CAT WITHOUT A FLOWER BOW?

I have to make Crinkles wear a flower on his collar. This is important. He cannot be a flower cat if he does not have a fancy flower—and it has to be big enough so everyone can see it.

I could make a flower out of paper, but I am lucky—I know someone who can make an even better flower than I can. That someone is Mimi.

I called Mimi the minute after I thought of how she could help me. Of course she said yes! That was the easy part. The hard part was going to be getting Crinkles to wear it.

That was going to take practice, and we were going to have to practice without Augustine Dupre seeing us.

SUNDAY

Today is Augustine Dupre's practice wedding. It is pouring rain! So far Mom has said "Poor Augustine Dupre" about twenty times.

The practice is at one o'clock. Mom says I'm not allowed to wear my new shoes in the rain, so I have been wearing them in the house all morning instead. I'm getting good! I've probably done about a hundred twirls, and now I don't even wobble or fall down at all.

I AM GOOD!

WHAT MOM FINALLY SAID YES TO

After I begged for about forty minutes Mom finally let me go downstairs to see if Augustine Dupre needed any help.

I did my special knock on the door. It sounded busy in there. I could hear a lot of people talking. After about five knocks Augustine Dupre opened the door and invited me in. The first thing I saw was Luke sitting on the sofa, and guess who was sitting on Luke? Crinkles! The second thing I saw was a little girl throwing pieces of paper all over the room. That kind of thing is hard not to notice—especially when it is handfuls at a time.

WHY AUGUSTINE DUPRE WAS HAPPY TO SEE ME

"Oh, Grace!" she said. "I'm so glad you're here. I want you to meet Delphine. She really needs your help." Augustine Dupre pointed to the little girl I had noticed already—now she was throwing handfuls of paper up into the air over her head. It was probably fun, but it certainly isn't what a flower girl is supposed to do.

Luke put Crinkles on the chair and stood up. He introduced me to everyone in the room—his parents, his aunt and uncle, and the little girl, who was of course Delphine. They were all French. I had to say a lot of bonjours.

FLOWER BASKET

CRUMPLED PAPER IS PRETEND FLOWER PETALS.

HOW I HELPED DELPHINE

Right away I could tell that Delphine liked me. Sometimes little girls like bigger girls, and lucky for me this was one of those times. I could also tell that we were not going to be super chatty together. Delphine only spoke French! I know a few French words like *bonjour, oui, non,* and *au revoir,* but you can't have a very big conversation if all you can say is hello, yes and no, and goodbye.

Augustine Dupre showed me exactly what Delphine had to do and then gave me a pot to use as my pretend bas- ket. That way Delphine and I could practice together.

POT ↓

FILLED WITH LITTLE PIECES OF PAPER ↙

WHAT IS REALLY FUN

I was surprised, but follow-the-leader-flower- girl is a pretty good game. After about fifteen minutes we were both excellent at it, and I was even wearing my fancy shoes!

STEP, THROW, STEP, THROW.

I could tell Augustine Dupre was super happy, plus she said, "Oh, Grace, you are the best!"

Crinkles was also super happy. He is not a big sit-on-people cat, so it was surprising to see him jump on Luke's lap whenever Luke sat down. Luke saw me watching. "I bribed him," he said, "with these." He held up a little can of cat treats. "Crinkles loves them! And now he loves me!" "Just like I do," said

Augustine Dupre. They looked at each other and smiled. It was a romance moment!

WHAT MOM WAS WRONG ABOUT

Augustine Dupre didn't seem one bit sad about the weather. The only time she even mentioned it was when I was leaving to go back upstairs. She said, "Grace, can you ask your mother if she has any extra umbrellas we can borrow for the rehearsal?" "Sure," I said, and I ran upstairs. I was in a rush. I needed to write down the name of those cat treats. They were going to be a big help!

THE REHEARSAL

I think rehearsals in the rain are probably much faster than rehearsals in the sun. The whole thing was over super quick. At the end, Mrs. Luther and Augustine Dupre gave each other a big hug. It was weird to see them be such good friends. I bet it was because of Crinkles.

THE TWO BEST PARTS

The FIRST best part was that I finally found out what my special wedding job is going to be, and I love it. It's super important. Mimi was 100 percent right: Augustine Dupre is good with ideas.

YOU WILL BE THE FLOWER GIVER.

YOU STAND AT THE ENTRANCE TO THE AISLE.

WHEN A PERSON COMES TO SIT DOWN, YOU GIVE THEM A FLOWER TO HOLD WHILE THEY WATCH THE WEDDING.

The SECOND best part of the rehearsal was that I could tell that if everything went perfectly right, my flower cat plan would actually really work. There was just one thing I needed to figure out. Sometimes when there is something you need to solve, it can help if you let the idea just sit in your brain for a while. Detectives do this when they are trying to solve mysteries. Mom loves to watch those kinds of shows on TV, so I know what I'm taking about.

MY LITTLE FLOWER CAT PROBLEM

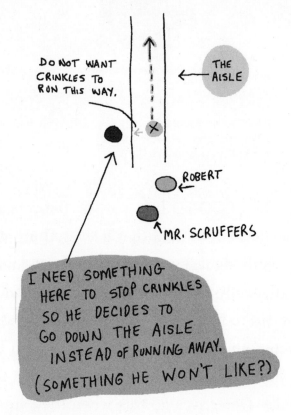

After the rehearsal, Augustine Dupre, Luke, and all the French people went to a restaurant. They invited me too, but Mom had already given me lunch, so I wasn't hungry. Plus I wanted to get Crinkles's flower from Mimi, go to the grocery store to buy the cat treats, and, if there was time, do another comic for Mr. Frank. My day didn't have any extra time for just sitting around!

WHAT WAS SURPRISING TIMES TWO

The first thing I did was ask Mom if we could go to the grocery store. Mom looked at me and said, "Are you reading my mind?" I shook my head. "Well, I was just thinking about asking you if you would mind coming with me to the grocery store."

Mom waited in the car while I ran upstairs to get my money. SURPRISE! You CAN buy a great wedding present for less than twenty dollars!

The second surprise was not so good. Cat treats can be really expensive, especially the ones that Luke had picked out. No wonder Crinkles liked them.

I told Mom I was getting Crinkles some treats so he could feel special on Augustine Dupre's big day. Mom smiled and said, "You're such a big animal lover. I'm proud of you." I didn't tell her there was more, and that I actually had a whole big wedding plan. Sometimes it's better and safer to keep some things a surprise.

MIMI'S CAT FLOWER

It was perfect! I loved it! For sure Crinkles wasn't going to love it. Hopefully I could help him with bribery!

SHE MADE A LITTLE PIECE ON BACK SO I CAN ATTACH IT TO CRINKLES'S COLLAR.

WHAT I REALLY HATE

Sunday spaghetti. Mom said I could just have butter and not eat the sauce. That was because Dad forgot that I don't like squash. Mom said that if I did like squash I would have loved it, because it was delicious! Mom was happy, Dad was happy, and because I didn't have to eat the squash, I guess I was happy too.

WHAT THERE WAS NO TIME FOR

I didn't have time to do another comic for Mr. Frank. Even though I had interviewed Dad and I had the idea in my head, there wasn't time to draw it. Sometimes not everything can get crossed off a list like you want it to be.

MONDAY

Not every day is exciting. Some days are just normal, regular days. Sometimes if you have had a lot of really busy days in your life, it's nice to have a regular day. Today was one of those.

THE BAD THING ABOUT TODAY

After school, I couldn't find Crinkles, and I really needed to start him on his flower-wearing practice! Sometimes when you put new things on cats they go all floppy and won't move. I know this because I once tried to have Crinkles wear a hat. He just fell on the floor and lay there like the hat weighed 1,000 pounds—which of course it didn't!

THE GOOD THING ABOUT TODAY

I finished another comic for Mr. Frank.

THE FLYING DONUT

TUESDAY

Tuesday starts with T and so does *terrific*! So far the comics club has done forty-three comics. That's amazing and terrific! They are not all excellent, but still, forty-three is a lot. Mr. Frank is even more excited about the project than he was last week. He said he is going to try to have the school let us have a special art show night with invitations and snacks and maybe even music.

WHAT CRINKLES CAN DO

Crinkles can be bribed with his favorite cat treats. After school I went looking for him. As soon as I saw him I shook the little can of treats. I'm lucky he is already trained about the sound. He knows it from Luke doing it, and today it worked like magic. He walked right up to me.

Crinkles was not excited about looking beautiful. As soon as I put the flower on his collar he flopped over onto his side and tried to get it off with his paws. I had to give him lots of treats to make him stop. Finally he sat up, probably because it was easier to eat the treats that way. My insides shouted, "Yay, Crinkles!" I tried to get him to walk, but he wouldn't do it. I put a treat down about a foot away from him, but he wouldn't stand up and walk over to it. I think he might have stopped being hungry. Next time I'd have to remember not to fill him up with so many treats right at the beginning. That and bring a camera. Mimi needed to see how cute he looked wearing her flower.

WEDNESDAY

Miss Lois doesn't care one bit that I have a lot of wedding planning to do. If she did she would not have given me so much homework. I told her I was too busy getting ready for Augustine Dupre's wedding to do three math pages tonight, but she didn't change her mind. "That's fine," she said. "Just bring a note from home if you can't do the homework." Mom is never going to give me a note. I bet Miss Lois knew that!

THE WEDDING PROBLEM SOLVER

I wasn't even thinking about my Crinkles wedding escape problem when I got the answer of how to fix it. It just popped right into my head. It wasn't going to be easy, but if I could get the right help, it would work. I was sure of it. Now all I had to do was to get Sammy Stringer to say yes. Hopefully he was like Crinkles and could be bribed too.

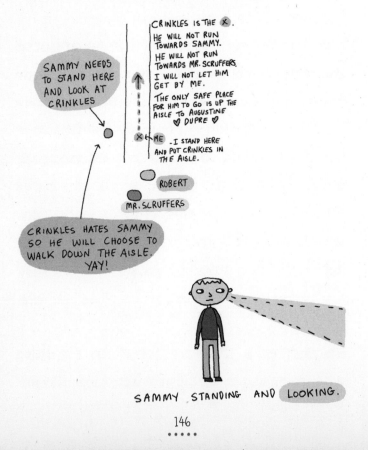

CRINKLES IS THE ⓧ.
HE WILL NOT RUN TOWARDS SAMMY.
HE WILL NOT RUN TOWARDS MR. SCRUFFERS.
I WILL NOT LET HIM GET BY ME.
THE ONLY SAFE PLACE FOR HIM TO GO IS UP THE AISLE TO AUGUSTINE ♡ DUPRE ♡

SAMMY NEEDS TO STAND HERE AND LOOK AT CRINKLES

ⓧ ← ME . I STAND HERE AND PUT CRINKLES IN THE AISLE.

ROBERT

MR. SCRUFFERS

CRINKLES HATES SAMMY SO HE WILL CHOOSE TO WALK DOWN THE AISLE. YAY!

SAMMY STANDING AND LOOKING.

WHAT SAMMY SAID

As soon as I asked him, Sammy said, "NO!"
It was a big no—the kind that seems like it
could never be turned into a yes, but I know
Sammy, so I tried again. "You won't have to
stand even close to Crinkles," I said. "Plus I'm
paying." "What kind of pay?" asked Sammy.
I quickly thought about my money at home
and how much I had left over. "Uh . . . four
dollars and twenty-six cents," I said. Sammy
thought for a moment. He shuffled his feet
then said, "Well, I do need to get more gum
for my project. Do you swear that the cat is
not going to come even close to me? "Not
anywhere near. Hand over my heart," I said.
"I swear!" "Okay," said Sammy, "I'll do it, but
don't tell anyone. I don't want anyone to see
me." He turned and started to walk away. I
ran after him. "And don't forget, you have to
wear the oven mitts!" "I know! I know!" said

Sammy. "And the other stuff too." I watched him go. I was happy . . . but wondering. Sammy is like that.

MAKING THINGS RIGHT WITH MAX

A good friend does not let a whole week go by without trying to fix a hurt friend's feelings. Even though Max and I are not best friends, we still see each other a lot, so him being mad at me was not good. I couldn't tell if he was still upset with me, so I was a little nervous when I went up to talk to him. Mimi said to be brave, so I tried that. "Be brave, Grace, be brave!" I said it to myself five times over so I could have more brave energy. When Max saw me he sort of smiled—so that helped too.

WHAT I ASKED MAX TO DO

I took a deep breath, closed my eyes for a second, and then said, "If you have time on Sunday, I really need help with Mr. Scruffers. I need someone to be in control of her at Augustine Dupre's wedding." Max smiled. "I'm really good with dogs," he said. "I can do it!" I was glad he said yes, and secretly double glad that he didn't ask for money.

THE TWO OTHER GREAT THINGS THAT HAPPENED TODAY

1. Five new people have joined the comics club. So far we have made fifty-three comics! Mr. Frank said that he is 100 percent sure that we will be able to get one hundred comics done!

2. During Flower Cat training today Crinkles walked six steps! Mimi has to fix the flower, though, because he pulled off one of the petals while I was trying to get it on his collar. He's fast with the claws!

THURSDAY

I forgot all about Mimi's allergies. She can't really touch stuff that has been near a cat. She was super nice about it, though, and asked her mom to fix the flower instead. Mimi's mom did a good job. It looks the same as when it was new.

SCHOOL

The good thing about school today was that it went by kind of fast. Miss Lois actually planned a pretty fun day for us. In two weeks we are going on a field trip to visit a historical (that means old-fashioned) town. We spent the whole day talking about olden times. For sure it's more fun to talk about olden times than it was to live in olden times. Life was not easy back then!

WHAT CRINKLES GETS TODAY

If Crinkles cared about that sort of thing, today would have been his gold star day! He was amazing. He walked all the way across the yard with his flower on, and didn't even stop once to try to scratch it off. Now I am really excited about Sunday!

FRIDAY

Today I had another good idea. I'm going to put Crinkles's favorite cat treats in the bottom of Delphine's flower basket. That way Crinkles will smell them on the flower petals she throws. Maybe that will make him go down the aisle easier. At first I thought Delphine could just throw some cat treats on the ground, but then I thought about Mr. Scruffers. For sure she would see them. I did not want her to be running down the aisle thinking we were playing some kind of cereal game. A good wedding planner has a lot to think about. It uses up a lot of brain power. I hardly had any left to listen to Miss Lois.

MOM'S GREAT IDEA

Mom said to invite Mimi over for a movie night. We got two movies and pizza and Mom even baked cookies for dessert. Augustine Dupre was having a party downstairs, but we were too busy to go down to visit her. Mom said it was probably a grownup party, but I know that Augustine Dupre doesn't care about stuff like that. She always likes to see me!

COOKIES   POPCORN   PIZZA

SATURDAY

The biggest, most important thing I have to do today is to practice with Crinkles one more time. We have been doing our practicing in the front yard, so I am hoping he will be out there again. Mimi said she is all ready for her part. Her job is to stand with Robert and make sure he doesn't eat his crackers too fast or drop them. It doesn't seem like a hard job, but it's a really important one. If something goes wrong with Robert, everything will be ruined. Mr. Scruffers won't sit calm and still, and Crinkles won't do his fancy slow motion walk down the aisle to meet Augustine Dupre. Just thinking about it made my stomach feel bubbly. More than anything ever, I wanted Flower Cat to work!

Mom could tell that something was up. She thought I was worried about my hand-ing-out-the-flowers wedding job. "You'll be great tomorrow, don't worry," she said. I tried to smile, but I could only do the not-real school one. It made her suspicious. "Grace, is there something else I should know about?" she asked. For a second I thought about telling her, but then I changed my mind. What if she said, "Absolutely not! You cannot do Flower Cat!" I did 100 percent not want that to happen, so I said, "No, nothing. Everything's fine." Somehow this made my stomach even more bubbly, and now I was getting a headache too. "Why don't you go outside?" said Mom. "Maybe you need some fresh air."

WHAT WAS HAPPENING IN MRS. LUTHER'S YARD

There were lots of people at Mrs. Luther's house. They were putting lights in the trees, setting up tables and chairs on the lawn, and unloading all sorts of boxes into the garage.

If there is lots of activity in the neighborhood, people notice and want to see what's going on. That's probably why Mrs. Witkins, Mr. Hurley, Max, Sammy, Mimi, and Robert were all standing on the sidewalk, watching. "I'm getting Robert used to the idea," said Mimi. "He's pretty excited." Robert nodded his head yes so that I'd know that Mimi was telling the truth. "So what exactly am I supposed to do tomorrow?" asked Max. "Let's talk now," I said. "I'll explain everything again."

The talk was a good idea. Now everyone knew exactly what they were supposed to do. Explaining things out loud is a good way to find out if there are any mistakes in your plan. It was the way I suddenly knew I had one big mistake in my plan, and it was about Crinkles.

WHAT I SUDDENLY THOUGHT OF

How was I going to find Crinkles at the exact time I needed him? What if he was nervous about all the people in the yard and ran off and hid somewhere? What if he stayed in Mrs. Luther's house and wasn't even outside? It was a big, horrible, ruin-everything problem that I had no idea how to fix! Lucky for me the no-idea part only lasted for about ten minutes. Fixing it wasn't going to be easy, but if I could use Augustine Dupre's brain-control trick, everything might still work out.

WHAT I SAID TO AUGUSTINE DUPRE

Augustine Dupre has empathy feelings for Crinkles. I know this is true, and I hoped those feelings were going to help me too. I watched for a second when she didn't seem too busy, and then I went over to talk to her. "Have you seen Crinkles?" I asked. "He probably doesn't like having all these people around. Do you think he'll get nervous and run away? Remember how he didn't like Mrs. Luther's cast? It's too bad that he can't just be somewhere nice and quiet while all this is going on tomorrow." I looked up, to see if my questions were working—to see if my brain was giving her brain an idea.

MY BRAIN GIVING AUGUSTINE DUPRE'S BRAIN AN IDEA

Augustine Dupre put her hands up to her mouth. "You're right, Grace," she said. "I haven't seen him. He won't like this." She looked over at Mrs. Luther's house and then looked at her apartment. Suddenly she smiled. "Wait," said Augustine Dupre. "Mrs. Luther's house isn't a good choice because there will be too many people going in and out of there preparing the dinner, but my apartment is quiet. Maybe he can stay there until tomorrow night, when it's all over. He likes it. It's safe." I clapped my hands. "That's a great idea," I said. "And I won't tell anyone." "Okay," said Augustine Dupre. "It's our little secret."

Then, right before I was about to leave, she said one more thing. "Do you think you could visit with him a little tomorrow—between the wedding and the dinner? I'll leave my door unlocked." She looked at me hoping I would say yes. "Of course," I said. "No problem." And then I smiled my 100 percent real smile, because suddenly I was 100 percent really happy!

For the whole rest of the day I was perfectly sure that everything was going to work out perfectly! But then something weird happened. As soon as nighttime came, all my good feelings faded away, just like the sun.

MY ALMOST LAST THOUGHT BEFORE FALLING ASLEEP

I should be careful and not give Mr. Scruffers very much cereal tomorrow morning when we play our game. That way she'll be extra hungry and concentrate extra hard when Robert eats his crackers.

MY LAST THOUGHT

I don't know if there is a job for people who plan wedding stuff, but if there is, that is not the kind of job I want when I grow up. It is way too filled with worries!

SUNDAY

I woke up extra early, even before Mr. Scruffers. We went downstairs like normal, but instead of it being seven a.m. it was six a.m. Mom must have been excited too, because she came down at seven-fifteen and she never gets up that early on Sundays. "How about some French toast?" she asked. It was the perfect thing for a day like today. I know it's probably not true, but I like to think that French toast gives me extra power, and today was definitely a day for needing extra power.

WHAT WAS BAD ABOUT THE MORNING

Waiting! It was super hard to wait for the wedding to start. Time seemed like it was moving as slow as on a boring school day. I couldn't find anything to do. Mom finally let me watch TV just so I would stop walking back and forth all over the house.

Mimi came over at about ten-thirty. "I can't wait for the wedding," said Mimi. "It's going to be great!" "Really?" I asked. "Of course," said Mimi, "and Augustine Dupre is going to love Flower Cat! Today is going to be the best day of her entire life. She gets to be married and get a super-amazing present, both at the same time." Mimi bounced up off the sofa. "Come on. Let's go check out the wedding." "Okay!" I said. It felt good to be doing something. I followed her outside.

MRS. LUTHER'S YARD

Everything about the set up for the wedding was beautiful. There were flowers and pretty white and yellow bows everywhere. It was amazing.

FLOWERS ON TREES

I was happy that the wedding aisle looked just like I thought it was going to, it made me feel better about my plan. There were three people still working and putting things together—two ladies and one man. They were really busy but didn't look unhappy or worried. Maybe I was wrong about the wedding planner job.

THE BEST THING ABOUT BEING IN MRS. LUTHER'S YARD

Watching everyone get ready for the wedding used up all the waiting time!

WHAT IS A GOOD IDEA

I was just about to rush home to get dressed when Mimi said, "Grace, wait! One more thing! Even though I'm not really invited to the wedding, do you think it's okay if I wear something nice?" "Oh, Mimi," I said. "That would be great." "Good," she said. "And don't worry, I'll dress Robert up too!"

WHAT WAS PERFECT

The twirl I did in my fancy dress right before I went outside to the wedding.

WHAT WAS A BIT OF A SURPRISE

I thought Augustine Dupre would be in Mrs. Luther's yard, waiting, but Luke said she wasn't going to come out until just before the wedding started. That way everyone could be surprised about how beautiful she looked. It was a great idea! I couldn't wait to see her walk down the aisle.

WHAT WAS NOT A SURPRISE

Delphine looked adorable! And she did not

notice at all when I put some of Crinkles's treats
in the bottom of her flower girl basket under all
the flower petals.

WHAT I WAS EXPECTING

Mimi, Robert, and Max were all waiting for
me by the big tree in my front yard, just like
we had planned. Mimi looked great. She was
wearing her favorite yellow dress, but my favorite thing was the little fancy bow tie she
made for Robert from one of her headbands.

MIMI'S HEADBAND

ROBERT'S BOW TIE

The only person who was missing was Sammy. At first I was nervous, but I looked down the street and way in the distance I saw someone waving. I could tell it was Sammy, but he was too far away for me to really see what he was wearing.

WHAT WAS A HUGE SURPRISE

Sammy up close!

I PICKED OUT MY MOM'S BEST OVEN MITTS BECAUSE IT'S A WEDDING.

CHRISTMAS PLATE TIED AROUND HIS MIDDLE LIKE A SHIELD

CHRISTMAS OVEN MITTS WITH SNOWMEN ON THEM.

MORE POT HOLDERS. THE SQUARE KIND.

WHAT I DID JUST TO BE SAFE

Right before the wedding started, I had everyone go over their jobs one last time. They all got A-pluses! Everything was going to be perfect!

MY FIRST WEDDING JOB

I was talking with Sammy when Luke suddenly appeared. "Are you ready?" he asked. I nodded yes. It was time to start my flower job. Luke took a second look at Sammy, but he didn't say anything. He was probably too shocked to speak.

I followed Luke down to the wedding chairs and took my spot right in the middle of the aisle. No one could get by without me giving them a flower. It was a fun job. The best part was that I got to decide which guests got which flowers. My favorites were the lilies. I only gave those to the ladies.

Some of the guests were people I knew, like Mom, Dad, Mrs. Luther, and Lily and her mom and dad, but most of them were strangers. Everyone was really friendly, though, and happy to take a flower. I think most of the people were French, because there were more *mercis* than *thank yous*.

MY SECOND WEDDING JOB

As soon as everyone was sitting down, Luke gave me the signal. The signal was pulling on his ear two times. Delphine's mom was standing there too, but really it was my job to tell Delphine to start her flower girl walking. I gave her a big smile and pointed to the front of the aisle where Luke was standing. Her mom said something to her in French. Delphine smiled at me and then she took her first step. I was hoping she was going to walk slow, like we had practiced, because I needed that time to get Crinkles. I watched her for two seconds, just to make sure she was okay, and then I turned to run to Augustine Dupre's apartment.

WHAT I WASN'T EXPECTING

As soon as I turned around, there was Augustine Dupre. She was standing right behind me! She looked like a princess! The most beautiful princess ever! But I couldn't stay to talk. "Bathroom! Emergency," I lied, and I raced off.

SHE LOOKS LOVELY

TWO THINGS I WAS GLAD ABOUT

That I had practiced with Crinkles—he was so good about putting his flower on! And that I had practiced wearing my new shoes—even walking fast, back to the wedding with Crinkles, my feet didn't hurt one little bit.

MY PRESENT FOR AUGUSTINE DUPRE

When I got back to Mrs. Luther's yard I could see everyone was in their right places: Sammy was at the end of the chair row so Crinkles could not escape, Max and Mr. Scruffers were at the start of the aisle, and Mimi and Robert were about two feet away from them.

I looked down the aisle and saw Augustine Dupre walking to the front—she was almost there. Everyone was looking at her. No one was even guessing what was about to happen. It was perfect, except for one thing. There were two people sitting in my way.

I was lucky—the two people were very nice. They made room for me to go by and didn't even complain. They were probably too surprised to talk. It's not every day you see a fancy cat at a wedding.

FLOWER CAT

Crinkles and I got into position. It seemed like forever for Augustine Dupre to get to the front. I waited for her to turn around so she could see Crinkles, but she didn't. And then the music stopped and everyone sat down.

Suddenly Crinkles decided to be super squirmy. I tried to give him one of his treats, but he didn't care about treats anymore. He tried to bite me. And then his claws came out! All of them! He was like a spinning piñata of needles. "Ahhh!" I screamed and pulled my hands away. I dropped him. He landed right in the middle of the aisle. I don't know if my scream was loud or soft, but suddenly everyone was looking at me. My face felt red and hot. And then, at least for me, everything was like a slow-motion movie.

THE SLOW-MOTION PART

I looked across at Sammy, and he was flapping his oven mitts just like he was supposed to. Crinkles was frozen. He was as still as a statue standing in the aisle exactly where I had dropped him—only his eyes were moving. I knew he was trying to decide what to do. *WALK UP THE AISLE! WALK UP THE AISLE!* My brain was screaming at him, but I didn't make a sound. Suddenly Augustine Dupre made a noise, kind of like a gasp. Crinkles heard it too. It was perfect. It was the magic sound he needed. He looked back at Mr. Scruffers and then with his slow, fancy footsteps walked toward his favorite person in the whole entire world. I held my breath. Everyone did. The only sound I could hear was Robert crunching away on his crackers.

Crinkles had only six or seven more steps to take before he got to Augustine Dupre. I was guessing that once he got to the front of the aisle he would run right past her and make his escape. It was too bad, but I knew there was no way he was going to sit quietly up there at the front right next to her while she got married.

Finally I took a breath, and then two seconds later, everything changed.

THE FAST-MOTION PART

Everything was perfect until Robert yelled the one word that ruined everything. "SQUIRREL!" Instantly the spell was broken. Suddenly Mr. Scruffers lunged down the aisle after Crinkles, or an invisible squirrel. She was barking like crazy, dragging poor surprised Max right up the aisle behind her. Lucky for me I caught her and scooped her up as she passed by. She stopped barking the minute I picked her up, but still it was a total disaster. Instantly I knew one thing—I was going to be in a lot of trouble. I had ruined Augustine Dupre's most special day in her entire life. I started to cry. I didn't mean to, but I couldn't help it. I felt awful. I looked up at Augustine Dupre so she could see how sorry I was, and there in front of me was the most perfect thing ever. I couldn't believe it. It was Crinkles in Augustine Dupre's arms. She must have caught him and picked him up.

WHAT HAPPENED NEXT

Everyone took tons of pictures of Augustine Dupre and Crinkles and Luke, and the funny thing about it was that Crinkles didn't seem to mind one little bit.

Finally Mrs. Luther came and got Crinkles and took him away so Augustine Dupre and Luke could get married. It was a beautiful wedding. I cried a lot. It was mostly happy crying. The lady next to me was really nice. She gave me at least five tissues, and whispered that her favorite part of the whole wedding was the cat part.

When Augustine Dupre and Luke were done getting married, they walked down the aisle together and everyone gave Augustine Dupre their flower so she could have a bouquet. When I gave her my flower she blew me a kiss. It made me cry again—good thing the lady was there with the tissues.

TEARS

TISSUE
FULL OF
TEARS

WHAT I DID NOT KNOW UNTIL THE VERY END

I was standing watching Augustine Dupre and Luke when someone touched my shoulder and said, "How did you do that?" I knew the voice. It was Dad. "How did you know that Crinkles would jump right into Augustine Dupre's arms?" He was standing next to Mom. They looked more surprised than mad.

"What a shock!" said Mom. "I knew you were up to something." She pointed her finger at me. "But still, you were lucky. It could have turned out differently. I'm not sure how I feel about the whole thing. I'll have to think about it." I put my head down. I wanted Mom and Dad to think I was feeling serious about what they were saying. I didn't want them to know that my brain was really thinking, *I CAN'T BELIEVE IT!!!!! CRINKLES JUMPED UP INTO AUGUSTINE DUPRE'S ARMS!*

Suddenly two arms grabbed me in a hug. It was Augustine Dupre. I could tell from her perfume. "Oh, Grace," she said. "You are just perfect! Thank you!" And then guess what? I cried some more!

SAD TEAR

HAPPY TEAR

THEY LOOK THE SAME BUT ARE COMPLETELY DIFFERENT.

FIVE THINGS THAT ARE GOOD TO KNOW ABOUT A WEDDING

1. Just because you are not invited at the beginning does not mean you won't get invited at the end. Augustine Dupre in-

vited Sammy, Mimi, and Robert to stay
for the whole rest of the wedding. I had
to change my dress, because it was covered in cat fur and I wanted to sit with
Mimi. It was worth it.

2. Being a flower girl helper can feel really
good.

3. You should never let a four-year-old be by himself near the wedding cake.

4. A boy who you think has bad manners might surprise you when he is somewhere fancy.

5. Good presents don't always come in wrapping paper.

TWO NEW GOOD THINGS

I was thinking that I would really miss Augustine Dupre while she was away on her honeymoon, but the truth is I've been pretty busy. She's been gone for a week, and I've hardly had time to feel sad. It's unusual for two surprising good things to happen on the same day. It was not something I was expect-

ing. My two new good things made me smile
from morning until night.

1. MR. FRANK SHOWED US OUR
   BOOK!

2. I GOT A POSTCARD FROM
   AUGUSTINE DUPRE!

Front of card

Back of card

Dear Grace,

I want to thank you again for the most wonderful wedding present. My special day was one hundred times more special because of your thoughtfulness. I cannot imagine how you were able to train Crinkles so well. You have a very nice group of friends and I want to thank them also. Both Luke and I feel very lucky to have you as our friend! Love and kisses, Augustine Dupré. xo

MY FAVORITE DAY

Mimi and I have a new favorite day—it's Flower Cat Friday. If Crinkles could understand it, I'm sure he would be proud!

OUR OUTFIT FOR EVERY FRIDAY

OUR SHIRTS LOOK GREAT.

A PEEK INSIDE *COMMUNITY COMICS*

Here are some of the comics from our book. I never knew there were so many different ways to play games. I'm going to try some of them. For once, something I learned at school was actually going to be helpful at recess.

MIMI'S COMIC

ABIGAIL'S COMIC

MARTA'S COMIC

SUNNI'S COMIC

A special thank-you to my comic artists.
Abigail's comic—Risa Liebmann
Marta's comic—Emily Michaels
Sunni's comic—Grace O'Rourke

Book
9